Remember
White Meidilands

Shirley Ann Gandy

PublishAmerica

Baltimore

ISBN: 1-4137-0182-5
PUBLISHED BY PUBLISHAMERICA, LLLP
www.publishamerica.com
Baltimore

Printed in the United States of America

For
Gary and Greg

Chapter One

Life was unfair. Most of the time. The exact moment she made that conclusion was unclear. It was a long time ago. Probably after one of her attempts to escape, or when she was forced to return defeated and ashamed. There was a way out. She just hadn't found it. But then, he wasn't bad all the time.

She pulled the two-wheel cart down the Chicago sidewalk, a trip she had made so many times she could almost find the store with her eyes closed. Thump, thump. The wheels bounced in rhythm. Her private hour. Time for plotting escape. Time for dreaming of a better life.

She enjoyed the first part of the trip. Pulling home a cart full of groceries beneath the July sun hanging at mid-afternoon would drain her energy. Her baby-blue cotton dress would be damp with sweat, her sandals would be gritty and she would be wondering how it would feel to own a car. Useless ponder, of course, a luxury she couldn't afford. Muse that brought to mind a scolding from Sister Evelyn at the orphanage when she had hitchhiked as a teenager.

"I know it was raining, you didn't have taxi fare and the driver was friendly. Count your blessings, young lady. You were lucky this time," Sister Evelyn had said. "You must never get in a car with a stranger. When will you learn to obey?"

Obey. Obey. Fifteen Hail Marys. Ten toilets. Seven days of silence. On her sixteenth birthday she was forgiven. She received an umbrella and a small purse for taxi fare.

One girl, who didn't learn to obey, wasn't so lucky. She hitchhiked and never returned. Sister Evelyn said the person who picked her up did awful things to her. All the girls joined hands in a circle and pledged to never hitchhike, never talk to strangers.

Be a good girl. Obey. Obey. She knew all about that. First the nuns. Then a boss. Later a controlling husband. Now, she was obeying for Sammy, the only good in her life. Someday she would be free and wouldn't obey anybody.

With her cart folded and placed under her grocery buggy, she walked up and down the aisles comparing prices and labels until her shopping list was complete.

Seeing a long line of buggies at the counter, she paused at the magazine rack where a man with a neatly trimmed beard was reading a Louis L'Amour paperback. His blue baseball cap with a white B on the front was pushed back showing his black curls. Hazel-green eyes peeked over metal-rimmed shades sitting low on his straight nose. He smiled at her without showing his teeth. She squatted and fumbled through magazines on the lower rack, observing the man from the bottom up. Long, slender legs ran up from blue Converse sneakers to cut-off jeans that hung around his flat belly where a blue, sleeveless t-shirt was partly tucked in. He wore a two-toned Rolex and a gold and black college ring.

Hmm. Dressed like a hobo. Expensive jewelry. Could be a thief, a drug lord, or an undercover agent. Her imagination was running wild as usual. She stood up, pushed her buggy to the counter and unloaded her groceries.

She read the cash register tape, counted money out on the counter. A quarter short.

"I thought I had another quarter." She dumped the contents of her purse on the counter, searching for change. *The regular cashier would let it slide until tomorrow.*

"Where's Janet?"

The new cashier shrugged.

"Here, let me." The bearded man gave the cashier a quarter.

"That's okay. I'll just put something back." She stuffed her belongings back in her purse and sat a can of soup on the counter. "It's too hot for soup anyway."

"This could happen to anyone." The man put the can of soup

back in her sack.

"Thanks," she said, embarrassed.

"No problem." He went to the end of the line and by the time he had made his purchase, she was gone. He had seen her in the market before, but didn't have a chance to get acquainted. Maybe he would see her on his next trip to Chicago.

Zack Cole preferred quiet country living to city life and a busy schedule only magnified his need for isolation. That's why he had carefully picked and trained trustworthy, top-notch managers for his offices in Chicago, Atlanta, and Dallas. From his Tennessee mountain home, he supervised his companies using high-tech computers and phone systems. When city meetings were absolutely necessary, he avoided downtown high-rise hotels with gyms and twenty-four/seven room service. He stayed in small motels on the edge of town where he could walk and jog in fresh air instead of using indoor treadmills.

A few years back, when his life rolled into a nightmare, he thought about dumping his fortune and sleeping in a cardboard box. Throw in the towel. Quit. Swim in bourbon until his nerves and thoughts were numb. He never made it to the cardboard box. After a week in the bourbon pool, he woke up and found the problems he had supposedly drowned still very much alive and growing into monsters that couldn't be bridled under a hangover headache. He came to his senses. Tried another approach. Work. Channeling his pain and anxiety into energy soon brought big business deals and more money than he knew what to do with. He had no personal life. He hadn't planned it that way. It was just the way it had worked out.

He checked in at the motel and had lunch with Dennis Wheeler, a sharp, smooth operator, who ran the Chicago office.

When Dennis joined the firm, he immediately picked up on Zack's exercise craze. From then on he showed up at meetings with his gym bag. Zack ignored the kiss-up technique. Dennis had potential. Three years with the company and he was handling the district so well Zack rarely came to Chicago. He was currently training a computer whiz kid to head the software division in the Denver office scheduled to open next month.

After lunch with Dennis, Zack went to his room, put on his cut-offs and jogged to the store where two months earlier he had given a quarter to the most beautiful woman he had ever seen. Though odds were slim that he would see her again, he looked through the store, then bought a bottle of water and headed for the park. From a block away, he recognized her straight, blond hair, hanging four inches below her shoulders, bouncing on her back as she pulled a cart full of groceries.

How lucky can a man be?

"We seem to keep running into each other," he said as he approached. "I didn't get a chance to introduce myself at the market. I'm Zack Cole."

"Hello, again, Zack Cole. Do you live in Chicago?"

"No. I'm here on business."

"I suppose you want your quarter back."

"What's a quarter between friends, Abby?"

"I didn't tell you my name."

"Didn't have to. I saw your I.D. when you dumped your purse on the counter at the market. You should be more careful with personal information."

"Are you a detective, or just plain nosey?"

"A little of both, I reckon."

"Then, I *reckon* you know everything about me."

"Abby Crowley, five-four, 110 pounds, blue eyes, blond hair, Landview Apartments, number A-3. Of course your birth date is another matter. I never mention a lady's age."

"Your memory is unbelievable. That was three months ago."

"More like two." *Hmm. She remembered.* "Point is, if I can get information so easily, so can criminals."

"How do I know you're not a criminal?"

"Do I look like a criminal?"

"Not exactly."

"How much further to your place?"

"You mean there's something you don't know?"

He moved out front and walked backwards so that he was facing her. A breeze blew her hair back revealing a bruise on her neck.

"Can we please start over? Our meeting like this seems like a miracle." *Right. Like you weren't looking for her.*

"So, you believe in miracles?" She stopped, stood still for a moment and couldn't help but smile. "You look ridiculous walking backwards. Get over here beside me like a sensible person." *Be careful. Obey. Obey. Never talk to strangers.*

He started walking beside her. "Is it always this hot in September?" *Dumb. You're here every September.*

"The humidity is what makes it so bad. There's a park ahead with shade trees where I usually cool off."

"I know the place." He lifted his cap and ran his fingers through his thick curls.

"I'm sure that beard doesn't help you stay cool."

"You don't like my beard?"

She smiled. Actually she loved his beard, but she wasn't about to tell him. "I hope it stays hot until Christmas."

"Are you saying you like hot weather?"

"Not really. When it's cold I can't take Sammy to the park. I used to bring him to the market. I'd load groceries around him in the stroller. He's too big for that now. And he's too small to walk this far."

"Who's Sammy?" he asked, though he was certain the toy truck in her buggy wasn't for a pet pigeon.

"My son. He's four, and a handful."

"That age can keep you hopping. Who's keeping him now?"

"My husband. Do you have children?"

"Nope. I was close to my friend's son until they moved to France. I visited him a while back. He'd grown so much I hardly recognized him."

"I know what you mean. Seems like yesterday Sammy was in diapers. There's an empty bench. Since I didn't buy anything that needs refrigeration, I'll rest a few minutes."

Nearby, an elderly man played with a small girl next to a picnic table where a group of women were deeply involved in a card game.

Abby took a slice of bread from the sack, tore it into tiny pieces and tossed it to the birds.

"I like to feed the birds. Bob says I'm wasting food."

"Huh," Zack said.

"Look how quickly they peck the crumbs. No matter how much I feed them, they always come back for more."

"It's been a long time since I've seen anyone enjoy such small pleasures."

"I didn't realize it was a small pleasure."

It is when your head's in a computer, your ear's to a phone.

"How long have you lived here?" he said.

"All my life." Before she knew it, she had told him about growing up in an orphanage eight blocks in the other direction, how she had married Bob and moved into the apartment where they still live. She even told him about the hitchhiking ordeal.

"I'll never again get in a car with a stranger," she said.

"That's good to know." He took off his shades and rubbed his hazel-green eyes. "Look. There's a couple of empty swings."

Soon they were swinging, letting the air cool their faces.

Two nuns and a group of children lined in a row marched from the sidewalk into the park.

"Amazing how they get kids to walk in such a straight line."

"You'd be surprised at the tactics nuns use to keep children under control. What's that tune you're humming?"

"Alan Jackson's *Little Bitty*," he said.

"Who's Alan Jackson?"

"You never heard of Alan Jackson? What kind of music do you listen to?"

"Whatever Bob plays."

"You gotta' try country."

"I've never given much thought to country twang."

"Country is America's music. Grabs the heart."

"Well, I guess I'll have to listen to country just to get my heart grabbed," she said.

Zack smiled. *Music, the universal language. Should I ask about the kid? Not unless you want the husband to move back into the conversation. Finally meet a captivating woman and she's married, with a kid.*

"This makes me feel like a teenager," he said.

"Well, teenager. What do you want to be when you grow up?"

"Clint Eastwood type. Mysterious, quiet, going around fixing other people's problems, knocking off the bad guys."

She dragged her foot to stop the swing. "What time is it?"

"Five o'clock. Why?"

"I'm late. Nice to see you again," she said, grabbing the buggy handle.

"Hey, wait a minute. What's your hurry? We're going in the same direction. I'll walk with you as for as your house."

"No! Just forget you ever met me."

"I'm afraid I can't do that," he said, puzzled.

"Then, stay away from me," she said.

"What did I do?"

"Nothing. You just don't understand," she said.

"No. I certainly don't."

How could she be full of life, in control, friendly one minute and terrified the next? Keeping distance between them, he followed and watched her enter a run-down apartment building.

Chapter Two

Zack's motel suite suddenly seemed small. During the night he had kicked the covers from the bed and moved around the room from chair to chair like a caged animal. He couldn't get Abby's frightened face off his mind. He looked around the room and shook his head. He was usually neat and orderly to a fault. Today, the maid would earn her money straightening his room. He showered and threw his towel on the floor. Being neat didn't make sense at this point.

Don't get involved. She's married with a kid. Your life is a mess already.

Reason and logic were getting in the way of his curiosity.

He was in no hurry to get back to Tennessee. He canceled his flight, told the desk clerk he was staying and walked across the parking lot to the diner. Rain during the night had cooled the air, but steam already rising from the pavement was a good indication that today would be another scorcher.

He sat at the counter sipping coffee, looking at the menu.

His friends used to say he could knock down brick walls without a bulldozer. A fix-it man. An expert at solving other people's problems. A master at covering up his own pain and self-inflicted guilt. That was all about to change and he knew it. The take-charge man was losing control, rolling down a hill, heading straight into a brick wall. What was worse, he didn't care. He had never walked away from a challenge and he wasn't about to start now. Abby needed help. He needed a plan. He dropped money on the counter and left.

In Abby's market, he bought a bottle of water, some birdseed and headed to the park. Consumed in thought, he started talking out loud.

"Why was she frightened? She's married, with a son—"

Realizing he was walking behind a gray-haired man in shorts, with tooth-pick legs and a little round belly, he said, "Good morning, Sir. I'm practicing my speech."

"Sounds like you're talking yourself into a heap of trouble. Is she worth it?" the old man said.

"You remind me of my dad. Ask one question and solve a problem. Thanks," he said and jogged on.

The park was quieter than yesterday. He scattered seeds and watched the birds peck cautiously. They had been more at ease with Abby.

"Scared, huh? Me too. Guess you'd rather have bread crumbs." They flew away when he moved to a shaded bench.

A child's cry took his attention to a woman changing a kid's diaper on a picnic table. She gently placed him in a stroller and soon they were out of sight.

There was that sound again. He turned and saw a man holding a stuffed monkey in front of a boy, who looked to be four or five years old. When the boy, dressed in shorts and sneakers, reached for the toy, the man pulled it back. The boy fell. It must have been going on for some time. The boy's knees were abraded.

"Stop whining like a baby," the man said to the boy.

Zack jogged forward and bumped into the man hard enough to knock him down.

"What the . . .? You'd better watch where you're going, buddy," the man said from the ground.

I will never be your buddy. I choose my buddies carefully. Zack picked up the monkey and gave it to the boy. "Here ya' go." The boy smiled at Zack with tear-soaked cheeks.

"Jerk," Zack said to the man and jogged away.

With Abby nowhere in sight, he returned to the motel, showered, laid back on the bed and surfed TV channels. Daily soaps dominated the networks. He chose a western on cable and soon dozed off.

He was in a forest. A bomb exploded. Or was it a gunshot? Abby's cry for help echoed in the distance. He was running, looking. She was nowhere. Then, she was in a hospital bed, calling his name. He kept running, but couldn't reach her.

He woke up in a sweat. This was one of those times when he remembered why he worked long hours, jogged to release tension, to forget. Now, there was Abby. So be it. He wasn't about to start ignoring his feelings this late in life.

He dressed and planned how he would go to the apartment, knock on the door and… pretend to be a salesman. Selling what? He could say he was looking for an old college friend. What if Abby answered the door and freaked out like she had in the park just before she rushed off? Could he take that chance? Of course not. He couldn't do any of that.

He started walking and found himself near Abby's apartment. It was a two-story job, with outside doors at each end of a hallway that ran through the middle of the building. Entrance doors to the apartments were staggered inside the hall.

He was leaning on a telephone pole when suddenly the outside door of the building flew open. A woman, who looked like Abby, fled through the dusk toward the park.

It was Abby. He ran after her. "Abby. Wait."

She stopped, whirled around. "What are you doing here?"

"Never mind. What happened to you?" Her face was bruised and her lip was bloody. "Did someone attack you?"

"I think I killed him. I had to get out of there."

Zack led her to a bench under a streetlight.

"Looks like somebody tried to kill you. Did someone break into your apartment?"

She jumped up. "I've got to go get Sammy."

"Wait. Sit back down and tell me what happened."

"I think I've killed my husband." She blew her nose into the shirt she was holding.

"Did he do this to you?"

"He was eating supper and I was ironing this shirt. All of a sudden he slammed his fist down on the table. Food and milk spilled all over the place. He said the meat was raw and he'd teach me to serve him food not fit for a dog. He asked where I was yesterday, said it didn't take three hours to buy a few groceries. When I said I stopped at the park, he hit me and I fell. I couldn't stand it anymore. I got up, grabbed the iron and hit him in the head. He fell. I only hit him once." By now she was crying so hard Zack could hardly understand what she was saying. "I know he's dead. Blood was starting to puddle on the floor around his head. I didn't even unplug the iron. What have I done? Sammy's still in there. I've got to go back."

"I'm calling the police." Zack pulled his cell phone from his pocket. "You don't have to live like this."

"No! They'll arrest me. I'll lose Sammy."

Think. Think. "Was Bob still on the floor when you left?"

"Yes."

"I'll go get Sammy. Wait here on the bench under the light. Don't leave. I won't have time to look for you when I get back."

"What if Bob's up? What will you say?"

"You let me worry about that."

"Be careful," she said.

"No problem. I've been through worse than this."

Yeah. Macho man. Flex your muscles.

He entered the noisy building and hurried down the hallway to apartment A-3. The door was ajar. Careful not to touch the knob, he pushed the door open, and closed it behind him with his elbow. He paused and scanned the room. A man was lying on the floor. The iron was burning the carpet. Keeping his eyes on the back of the man's head, he sat the iron on the board and jerked the cord from the wall socket. He grabbed a towel from the laundry basket and wiped fingerprints off the iron handle.

He reached to feel the man's pulse. *The jerk from the park. Finally got what you deserve.* First, the only pulse he felt was his own, pounding like a drum. Then, bloop, bloop, a soft beat.

He tiptoed through a door where a child lay sleeping with a stuffed monkey beside him in a bunk bed. *Sammy.* He lifted the monkey and Sammy, who must have remembered him from the park. He opened his eyes, smiled and leaned into Zack's chest.

Making his way across the room, he stepped over Bob, closed the door behind him and headed down the hall. Two teenagers were so caught up in music from their blaring radio they didn't notice him. As he reached the end of the hall, a woman opened her door and picked up a cat.

"Kitty-cat," Sammy said.

Zack turned so the woman couldn't see his face. "Does your monkey have a name?" he whispered.

Sammy shook his head no.

"Well, we can't have a monkey without a name. Let's call him Willard. Okay?"

"What's your name?" Sammy whispered, like Zack was doing, like it was a game.

"I'm Zack. What's your name?" *As if I didn't know.*

"Sammy."

"I'm taking you to your mama, Sammy. See? There she is."

Abby jumped up from the bench. "Was Bob . . .?"

"He's alive. Let's get you situated in a safe house."

"No. I've tried that and you see where it got me. I'd rather sleep on the street."

"You can't do that. How about the orphanage? The Sisters?"

"Tried that, too. It's the first place he'll look. You've done enough. I'll be okay."

"Not out here, you won't. I'm taking you to my motel room."

"Oh, no you don't. I've heard about men like you."

"You and Sammy can have a room to yourself."

"I don't have money for a room."

"No problem," he said. *I'm going to help you whether you like it or not.*

He led her to the street and hailed a cab.

The air had finally cooled. Across the horizon, a million stars and a pale moon hung over Chicago's night sky, oblivious to the madness of the world below.

Chapter Three

Zack woke up at 6:00 a.m. when the sun peeked through a crack between the curtains and hit him in the face. The dark red flowers on the drapes stared at him, reminding him of the blood on the floor around Bob's head. He shifted in the chair where he had tried to sleep during the night.

Instead of sleeping in the room he had rented for her, Abby and Sammy had piled in his king-sized bed where they watched movies until they fell asleep around midnight. He had thought about sleeping in the other room, but decided to guard his visitors. Maybe he was worried that she would have a weak moment and return to the scene of the crime.

Nobody could have convinced him a week ago that he would be hiding a woman and child. To top it all, it had been his idea and beat anything he had ever done. His every thought took him deeper into a maze. He needed to find a solution before this trip to Chicago turned into a bigger circus than it already was.

When he went out for snacks the night before, he had called an ambulance for Bob. He didn't tell Abby. He wanted to see how she felt after a good night's rest. She had probably been right about not involving the police. The problem was easily solved by leaving. But, where did it go from here? The macho side of him said, *You've never been afraid to take chances.* His logical side said, *You'd better have a good plan.*

He had learned about abuse in Dallas when his company got involved with a women's crisis center. In some cases, after the center helped victims get free, they returned to their abusers, afraid they couldn't make it on their own. Especially when children were involved.

In most cases, abusers would threaten to take the kids to keep their victims in line. Abby apparently fit both categories, since she had left and returned before. Now he understood her mood change. A spunky, in control attitude was her way to shine when she wasn't around her abuser, a screen to hide her trapped, helpless feeling. He knew women like that in east Tennessee. They started out innocent, unsuspecting. They became tough, hard women, facing what they had to in order to survive, or keep their family together.

Tennessee. No one will know to look for Abby there. She needs to get out of Chicago. Now, there's a plan.

He quietly went to the bathroom, brushed his teeth, then wrote a note: "Be back soon. Don't leave. Zack." He sneaked through the room, propped the note by the phone, put the 'do not disturb' sign on the door and left.

The hospital was busy with nurses scurrying about, mumbling to one another, leaving the computer behind the desk unattended. Zack was bent over scanning the list of patients on the screen when a nurse resembling his military sergeant approached and spit out words that sounded more like a command than a question.

"May I help you, Sir?"

"I hope so. I'm looking for Cromwell, accident victim. Came in last night."

"Let me see," she said, taking over the computer. "Sorry. There's no Cromwell."

"How about Annette Crosby? I think she was in the same car," he said, stretching to see the screen as the nurse scrolled down the list of patients.

"Crosby? What was that first name again?"

"Annette," he said, as his eyes grabbed the information he wanted from the screen: Bob Crowley, room 218.

"Sorry. Not here," the heavyweight said and picked up a ringing phone. "Second floor, nurse station."

The halls reeked with alcohol, cleanliness and medicine, all familiar to Zack. He pushed the thoughts to the dark corner of his mind where they belonged and hurried down the corridor. He paused at the open door before stepping in. The ward had four beds, two on each side. The first bed on the right was empty. In the other was a young man with his leg in a cast. On the left side of the room, there was a white-haired man in the bed next to the window. The curtain was half-drawn around the other bed. Zack moved so that he saw Bob sleeping like a baby with a small bandage on his head.

He looks comfortable enough. Funny how some people are so hard to kill. At least Abby won't be charged with homicide.

At the Airport, he bought two tickets to Knoxville on his flight, then picked up a few items from a drug store and headed to the motel.

Careful not to wake Sammy, Abby got out of bed and read Zack's note. *Obey. Obey.* She dialed her home number. No answer. Should she call the police? Hospitals? Maybe she shouldn't do anything.

Sammy got up and went to the bathroom, then climbed up beside her on the love seat.

"I like it here," he said to his mother.

She turned on the TV and stopped on a channel where Tweety Bird was doing his thing, entertaining Sammy. She almost jumped out of her skin when a key turned in the door.

"Hello, sleepy heads. Here, Sammy. A friend for Willard. His name's Harvey," he said and gave the stuffed, white pony to the boy.

Abby jumped when someone knocked on the door.

"It's room service. I ordered breakfast."

A young man came in and put a tray on the table. After Zack signed the ticket, he said, "Have a good day," and left.

"I didn't know what you like. I got some of everything."

"I see that. Neither of us is picky when we're hungry. Do you always think of everything?"

"I'm working on it. Which brings up another subject. Do you want to see a doctor? About your bruises? For evidence."

"What evidence?"

She put a pillow under Sammy so he could reach the table.

"Just a precaution."

"I don't have insurance."

"We can get around that," he said, pulled out a chair for her and poured coffee. "I may have a solution to your problem. Why don't you and Sammy come home with me?"

"Where's home?"

"Tennessee," he said, watching her examine the make-up and sunglasses in the bag from the drug store.

"Do I need make-up?"

"It's medicated. For the bruises."

"You want us to go to Tennessee?"

"Why not? You can stay at my place until you decide what to do next. It's the perfect place to hide."

"Hide?"

"It's a figure of speech. City slickers spend weekends in mountain hideaways. People who live where it gets real hot have summer homes there. It's the perfect solution for your problem. We can be there by midnight."

She frowned and didn't say anything.

"I wasn't sure how you'd feel. I bought round-trip tickets. You can go visit a few days, come back when and if you want to."

Obey. Obey. Never talk to strangers. That's silly. I'm grown up, with a kid. Shed the childhood commands. Can I trust Zack? Didn't he save me last night? Hasn't he been a perfect gentleman? I've known him only a short time, but feel safer with him than ever before. Is it a sin to let a stranger help? He doesn't seem like a stranger. Maybe this is my ticket out. The escape I've waited and prayed for.

"Why are you doing this, Zack?"

Beats me. Just crazy I guess. Other than the thought of someone hurting you and Sammy puts murder in my mind and confuses me until I don't know what I'm doing.

"You need a place to stay. I've got a big, empty house."

"Like I said last night, I've left before. Once, I left Sammy at the orphanage with the nuns. While I was looking for a job, Bob found him and took him home. I had to go back."

"Do you have relatives in Chicago?"

"I don't have relatives anywhere that I know of."

"Then, you have no reason to stay here."

"Maybe I should go."

She got up, went to the window, pulled the curtains back and looked out. "This may sound like a lie to someone like you, but I've never been outside the Chicago area."

"I don't think you'd know how to lie, Abby."

"Are you sure it won't be a bother?"

Am I sure? A bother? Of course not! I'll just open myself up, allow you to get a good choking grip.

"I wouldn't have bought tickets if I weren't sure." He spread strawberry jam on toast and gave it to Sammy.

"I like Harvey." With the white horse in one arm and the toast gripped in his mouth, he climbed up on Zack's lap.

Thoughts swirled in Abby's head. If she stayed, she'd wind up with Bob and he'd be meaner than ever, now that she'd defended herself. If he died, she'd go to jail. What would happen to Sammy? But, could she just leave with someone she hardly knew?

"Maybe I should go to the shelter where I went before. But, if Bob dies, I'll be charged with murder. If I go with you, they can't find me. God. What have I done?"

"Abby, Bob's okay. He's in the hospital."

"He is?"

"I called an ambulance last night when I went for snacks. This morning while you were sleeping I went to the hospital. Bob's a big boy. He can take care of himself. You and Sammy don't have to live like you've been living."

"What's it like at your place?"

"I live in the Cherokee National Forest. There are lots of trees and wild flowers blooming all over the place. Wild animals wander in my yard."

"What kind of wild animals?"

"Deer, rabbits, squirrels, chipmunks, ground hogs. You'll just have to see for yourself. No words can describe it."

"I'll need a job. I don't have much working experience."

"Right now you need to clear your head."

"Like all men, you know exactly what I need."

"Not really. I'm just offering a solution to a problem that needs solving. You can stay at my place as long as you want to."

"What if Bob dies?"

"Bob's too darn mean to die." He looked at his watch, took the tickets from his briefcase and gave them to Abby. "If you need to think, you can stay here."

"I don't have money for this room."

"It's paid for." *Not entirely true, but it will be if you need it.* "I know it seems like a big decision." *Especially when someone's been making decisions for you.*

"I still don't know why you're doing this."

I'm a good guy. Gullible. Dumb. Now, there's a word.

"Good deeds have a way of coming back. Or, that's how it's always worked for me."

"How long do I have to think about it?"

"As long as you need. You have the tickets. You have a room. If you don't want to come now, you can come later. If you want to go on my flight, it leaves in two hours."

"Flying off with a stranger. What would the nuns say?"

"What do they say about the way Bob treats you, the way you've been living?"

"That I need to work on my marital problems. Divorce isn't in their vocabulary."

"I think you should do what's best for you and Sammy."

"I agree. I'll need to go home and pack some things."

"Going back to the apartment might not be a good idea. We can buy what you need when we get to Tennessee."

"Must I keep repeating myself, Zack? I don't have money."

"I'll loan you some money."

"Okay. I'll go and stay until I clear my head and get a job. Then, I'll pay you back every cent, plus the quarter."

"You've got a deal."

That precious quarter that brought us together.

He picked up the phone, told the desk clerk he was leaving and needed transportation to the airport.

Chapter Four

Abby sat by the window and watched Chicago grow smaller as the plane soared upward. Soon clouds became a white floor meeting the blue horizon, separating them from the world below, a world where she grew up and might never see again.

Had she ever loved Bob? Or, did she marry from a need to belong to a family? She honestly didn't know how she felt then. She had grown to hate life with him enough to defend herself. That was enough to think about for now.

Her whole outlook had changed in the last two days. Zack was proof that there was a world out there somewhere with good in it. That knowledge had given her the courage to stand up for herself. So, here she was, going to Tennessee with an almost stranger, who didn't seem like a stranger at all. For the first time in her life, she had hopes for a good future. She was excited and could hardly wait to get to his place. It sounded like Heaven. Peaceful, quiet—nothing but happiness. She hadn't felt safe in a long time. Safe felt good. Bob would never in a million years know to look for her in Tennessee.

Sammy was wearing earphones, watching a movie. He was quiet, except for an occasional giggle, or outburst. "Look, Zack. Look Mommy," he would say and point to the screen. When the movie ended, he leaned on Zack's shoulder and fell asleep.

"Sammy seems to like flying," Zack whispered to Abby.

"He seems to like you," she said.

"There's good music on channel seven."

"Country I suppose," she said.

"Actually, it's easy listening."

Soon, the music and the hum of the plane's engine lulled her to sleep.

Zack couldn't imagine such naivety in Chicago. City girls were supposed to be worldly. Though she seemed frail, she had to be pretty tough to have lived like that. He leaned back, closed his eyes and let his thoughts wander. If she had been happy with a good husband, he would have walked away. He hated to think what would have happened if he had not been outside the apartment that night. Would she have gone back to get Sammy, felt guilty, nursed her abuser back to health? Probably. He was glad he was outside that building. Being involved with Abby and Sammy had brought him back to life. He felt warm all over looking at her in the thin, blue dress with tiny yellow flowers, green leaves. She would need rugged clothes for mountain life.

The captain's voice on the intercom announced they were approaching the Knoxville Airport. Zack shook Abby's shoulder and pointed through the window to the city below. Minutes later, they were in the parking area.

"Somehow, I thought you'd have a bigger car," Abby said as Zack unlocked his white Ferrari.

"You want to go to the mountain tonight? Or, get a room and head out fresh in the morning?"

"How far is it?"

"A couple of hours. I say hours instead of miles, because ten miles on mountain roads can take thirty minutes."

"If you feel like driving, I'd like to go on. I got plenty of sleep on the plane. I guess you can tell I'm excited. This is my first real vacation."

The car darted through traffic and soon they were outside Knoxville going west on Highway 411. They turned south on Highway 68 in Addisonville and headed toward the mountains where the road became narrow, steep and curved and the thick woods came right up to the deep ditches.

"Does anyone besides you live in this wilderness?"

"You'd be surprised at the houses hidden in these woods."

"Really? Where?"

"See the little roads leading off the main highway? There are houses back in there. You can't see them until the trees shed their leaves in the fall and winter."

"How do people make a living around here?"

"Small factories, businesses. A lot of pensioners and retirees looking for peace and quiet in their latter years move to Soda Creek because it's economical. It's very different from Chicago. People help if you need them. Otherwise, you don't know they're around. You get all the privacy you want or need," he said and pulled off the road at a country store.

"This is the first sign of life I've seen for miles."

"It's the only service station and convenient store for miles in either direction. They also have bar-b-que, burgers, ice cream and such," Zack said.

She noticed the cultural difference when the man spoke.

"Ya'll jus' in time, Zack. I'z a fixin' to close 'er up."

"Glad I caught you. Fill it up, please, while I use your phone," Zack said, and stepped inside to call his caretaker.

"Is it business folks you bringin' in?" Oliver said.

"It's a lady-friend and her four-year-old son. Prepare the downstairs guest rooms. We'll be there in a few minutes."

"I see. We'll put sandwiches in the refrigerator. You want Minnie to come in tomorrow?"

"Same as usual," he said and hung up.

Further in the mountains, amid patches of fog, the car zig-zagged upward on a steep, cliff-like, narrow, gravel road.

"Are you sure you know where you're going? This road looks too steep to drive on," Abby said, feeling a little nervous for the first time since she had met Zack.

"Everyone has that reaction at first. I live on top of this mountain. It's about a mile high."

"It's very dark up here. The street lights are off."

"There are no street lights in the country," he said, almost laughing. "I can see this is going to be an adventure."

He drove upward on the narrow road through dark woods to a

26

dead-end where a road led to the left, another to the right.

"Oliver and Minnie live over there," he said, pointing to the left. "They look after my place while I'm out of town. You'll meet them tomorrow. I'm here on the right."

He pushed a button on a mechanism attached to the car's sunvisor that opened an iron gate, and drove down a driveway lined on each side with perfectly shaped evergreens. The car's headlights beamed on a huge log home. He pushed another button on the sunvisor that opened a garage door where he pulled the Ferarri in beside a red Isuzu Rodeo 4X4.

"It's chilly up here," Abby said, rubbing her bare arms.

"It gets cool up here at night."

He carried Sammy across a yard of thick grass and up steps on a banistered porch that ran around the house.

"What's all those lights down there?"

"That's houses. The ones you couldn't see from the road in the valley," he said.

She ran to the edge of the yard.

"It's looks like a sky above, another below," she said. The sound of a hoot-owl sent her running to catch up with Zack, who was now laughing.

"What was that?" she said.

"Just an old hoot-owl. He's completely harmless. You'll get used to sounds of wild birds and animals. They're more afraid of you than you are of them."

"I doubt that," she said and followed him through the door into a long room with a six-foot, stone fireplace in one end.

"Oh, my. This takes my breath away," she said.

"Oliver said Minnie would put sandwiches in the fridge. You can get them out if you want to, while I put Sammy to bed."

"That's okay. I'll just go with you."

She followed to a bedroom where moonlight glowed through a window with calico curtains pulled to the sides. Without turning on a light Zack put Sammy in a twin bed and covered him with a quilt that matched the curtains.

"You can sleep next to Sammy on the other twin bed. Or, if you prefer, there's a queen bed in this room across the hall. The bathroom is here between the two," Zack said, as they went to the kitchen.

"I've never seen so much wood," she said.

"All wood. Logs on the outside, cedar and white pine paneling inside."

"A mansion made of wood, in the woods. This room is three-in-one—a kitchen, dining, and living room with the biggest fireplace I've ever seen."

"I like open space," Zack said.

"How did you find this place?"

"A newspaper advertisement. When I saw the land, I knew this was where I wanted to live the rest of my life. Next thing I knew, I'd bought half a mountain and was building this house."

"You bought half the mountain?"

"The other half is the Cherokee National Forest, belongs to the government."

"You built this house yourself?"

"Most of it."

"It's really beautiful. Why did you build such a big house for just you?"

"That's a long story and tonight's not the time to get into it. You can sit here," he said, pulling out a stool at the breakfast bar. He put the tray of sandwiches on the counter, poured iced-tea, and then took a stool opposite Abby.

"I'm glad I went in the market last Thursday," he said. "Even gladder that you came to Tennessee."

"Me too," she said.

"Strange how you can spend years with a person and hardly know them, while others seem like old friends the first time you meet. I feel like I've known you for years. Being with you is so comfortable, it scares me." *Don't get too comfortable.*

"I know what you mean. Though I can't help but wonder what tomorrow will bring. What am I going to do? What will happen to Sammy and me? I can't pretend everything is okay."

"Slow down. You just got here."

"I can't get it off my mind. How am I supposed to give Sammy a better life? I can't take care of myself. I have very little education and job experience."

"You have plenty of time to make those decisions. Put it out of your mind and try to enjoy yourself."

"I don't know if I can, with so many unknowns. If it were just me, I could fly away without a care in the world. But I have Sammy to think about."

"Sammy's all the more reason to take your time, make the right decisions."

"That makes sense. Isn't there a law against what I did? Can they put me in jail or something?"

"You were defending yourself. Even if Bob were dead, which he isn't, no one would blame you. Sooner or later, Sammy would have become a target, too," he said, thinking about the park. *Bob was already abusing Sammy and you didn't even know it.*

"I keep wondering if someone will be hunting me."

"If anyone hunts you, which I doubt, they'll never know to look here. Somehow, it just seems right."

"I feel the same. All of this is so new and wonderfully exciting. Still, it's a bit frightening."

"You and Sammy are safe. That's all that matters."

He left the room and returned with a shirt.

"Here's one of my T-shirts for you to sleep in. Sorry, I don't have anything more appropriate."

More appropriate? I can show you more appropriate. I have an attic full of more appropriate. Not really. Wrong size. Too big. Want to see all the pretty clothes up there?

"Thanks. This will be fine," she said.

"I'll be in the room up these stairs if you need me. Sleep late tomorrow if you feel like it. I'll fix breakfast when you get up. Goodnight," he said and went up the stairs.

"Goodnight, Zack," she said. "And, thanks."

She went to her room, locked the door and laid in the twin bed next to Sammy, wearing her clothes, not his shirt. She was so excited she could hardly stand it. Yet, she was afraid to close her eyes.

Chapter Five

The digital clock by the bed said 9:00 a.m. Abby looked around the room and finally remembered where she was. When she saw Sammy's bed empty, she was not the least bit worried. No doubt he was with Zack. She stretched, got out of bed, and stood where the sun had warmed the Wedgewood blue carpet in front of the window. She wondered how many different type trees were in the crowded forest.

Turning toward the door, she saw a pair of jeans and a red-plaid, flannel shirt draped over a chair next to a pair of brown, leather boots on the floor. Deciding the clothes were for her, she put them on. Everything fit perfectly.

She went to the front room and wondered if Zack and Sammy were up the stairs by the kitchen where Zack had made his exit the night before.

She yelled, "Zack. Sammy. Anybody home?"

With no answer, she climbed the stairs, counting, one, two, three . . . ten. Through the open door at the top was the biggest bedroom she had ever seen. It was almost as big as her entire apartment in Chicago. Plush, green carpet was topped with over-stuffed, white, leather chairs. A green and white spread covered a king-sized bed that swung on chains from the ceiling. A computer sat on a wide desk by a sliding glass door that led out on a balcony over the front porch. She leaned on the rail beside a small green table and chairs and inhaled the fresh morning air. Beyond the valley, rows of mountains folded into layers as far as she could see.

This is awesome. I'm standing on top of the world.

On the opposite side of the bedroom was a bathroom with a huge sunken tub and double lavatories. The window overlooked stone steps that led down behind the house to a crystalline lake. *Breathtaking. This is a dream world.*

She opened the window and yelled to Zack and Sammy coming up the steps. Rushing downstairs and through the house, she went out to the edge of the front yard where a light breeze rustled through the spruce. Small, low, white clouds, that seemed almost close enough to touch, floated across the sky, casting shadows like dark spots on the thick green lawn.

"How long have you two been up?" she said to Zack coming across the yard with Sammy on his shoulders.

"Since dawn. I see the clothes fit," Zack said.

"Where did they come from?"

"Sammy and I went shopping. Did you find our note?"

"No. I was busy exploring the house."

"Look, Mommy." Sammy pointed to a squirrel scampering up a tree. "It's a squirrel. Zack told me."

She followed Zack across the front yard and down steps through an archway covered with pink, climbing roses. The second level was an array of yellow, red, and white roses bordered by an assortment of flowers, every color imaginable.

"How beautiful. Did you plant these?" she said.

"I planted the roses. Most of the bordering flowers are wild. When I moved here I found that working in the soil was relaxing. Roses have always intrigued me. Their beauty invites. Their thorns challenge. I chose Meidilands because they're good ground cover and flourish in this area with very little care and require no pruning. There are five types of Meidilands here," he said, proudly showing off the beauties. "The pink ones with singular blossoms, have red hips in the fall. The Scarlet is full-petaled and grows about three feet high. The Bonica is the only shrub rose to win the coveted All-American Selections Award. They're a nonstop factory of pink, carnation-like flowers, which, in test gardens out-bloomed their neighbors. In the fall, their red hips are darker than the others. The yellow ones seem almost florescent and compliment the others. The pure, cool, whites are my favorite. With thick, multiple petals, they look like snow all summer. They're two feet high, the lowest hedge of them all. That's why I put them on the outside of the landscape."

"I see what you mean. Strange how they stand out against all those colors. Now I understand what you meant when you said no words could describe this place. I honestly didn't know places like this existed."

She followed him back up the steps to the first level and sat down at a white, wrought-iron table.

"I left the wild flowers around the edge of the yard to prevent soil erosion and to insure that something is blooming almost year round. Those short plants are wild orchids. They bloom only once in the spring. The bushes with shiny, green leaves are Rhododendrons. In April, May, and June, they turn this slope into a red, white and pink floor."

"I would never have thought you were a gardener."

"Wait'll you taste my cooking." He grinned, then pointed at Sammy chasing a butterfly. "Sammy, don't go near the edge of the yard." He clipped a white Meidiland, took the thorns off and gave it to Abby. She immediately put it to her nose.

"The whites are my favorites, too. Their fragrance is wonderfully refreshing. Sweet, yet strong."

"Stay and relax. I'll be right back."

He returned with a napkin tucked in his belt, and a tray of dishes, coffee, orange juice, cheese omelets, toast, blackberry jelly and peach jam. "Let's eat," he said and lifted Sammy into the air, making him giggle before putting him in a chair. "I think I have a high-chair in the attic that will fit you."

"You have a high-chair in the attic?" Abby said.

"I'm hungry," Sammy said.

"Minnie made the blackberry jelly. I made the peach jam from my trees out back. They have white meat and make the best peach cobblers you'll ever taste. I've got some in the freezer. I'll whip up a cobbler for Sunday dinner."

"You're a great cook. Is there anything you can't do?"

"There's not much anybody can't do if they set their mind to it," he said, and started gathering the dishes.

"I'll do the dishes," Abby said.

"We'll do them together. Then we'll go exploring."

With Sammy on Zack's shoulders, they hiked through the forest on a narrow path until they came to a huge oak. Mother Nature had bent the bottom limb into a bench. They sat down for a moment to rest, listening to a waterfall in the distance. From there they climbed upward on rock steps until the path widened into a stone floor where a cool mist from the waterfall filled the air.

Abby sat near the edge of the cliff. She pulled off her boots and soaked her feet in the cold puddle that had formed from the waterfall's backdraft.

On the way home, Zack told stories he had learned from Oliver and locals. They came to several rock graves that belonged to Cherokee Indians who had died marching the trail of tears when white men drove them from the mountains. White men often married Indian maidens. Once they were married, her land became his, but her family was allowed to stay on the land. One Indian Chief was desperate to stay in his beautiful Cherokee Mountains. He broke his only daughter's heart by giving her in marriage to a white merchant. She loved an Indian brave and he loved her. To prove he loved the chief's daughter more than the white man, the brave dove to his death from where Abby had sat on the cliff. Though she was married to the white man, the chief's daughter came to Soda Creek waterfall every day and finally grieved herself to death. Her only child by the white man was Oliver's grandmother.

"I was sitting on sacred ground," Abby said.

"Yes, you were," Zack said.

A mother deer and two fawns leaped across the path.

Sammy said, "Look. Rudolph."

Zack laughed. "Rudolph has a red nose and antlers. Maybe these are his sisters."

It was almost dusk when they saw the house top protruding through a haze. When Sammy was finally asleep in bed, Abby joined Zack in the kitchen.

"I don't understand why Sammy was tired. He rode on your shoulders most of the day," she said.

"Learning is hard work for children."

"For adults, too. I ache in muscles I didn't know I had."

She sat down at the breakfast bar. "Can I help?"

"No thanks. You might want to go freshen up for dinner."

After a long, soothing shower, she dressed in a soft blue, silk lounging outfit that had been spread out on her bed.

"You really didn't have to buy all these clothes, Zack."

"My pleasure," he said.

"You'd better watch it. I could get used to this."

"I hope you do," he said.

"It's amazing how I keep finding a view of the mountains I haven't seen before," she said.

"That's one of many things I love about this place. The view stays the same, yet, it seems to change."

"Your decorator must have cost a bundle."

"Not really. I did most of it myself. The food's ready."

There really is nothing he can't do.

During the next few days, Sammy played so hard he no longer needed to be coaxed to sleep. He liked Oliver and Minnie. He clung to Zack. He cried for the first time when Abby forced him to leave Zack alone to work.

Zack finally came down from his office and said, "I'll be gone about three days. Anything you need from the city?"

"What city?"

"Atlanta, Dallas."

"Is that where you work?"

"I work wherever I am. Make yourself at home. If you need anything, tell Oliver or Minnie. She'll be here every day to clean and cook."

"Zack, I can cook and clean."

"You might enjoy Minnie's company. She'll introduce you around the neighborhood, if you feel like making friends. Here are the keys to the Ferrari. It's in the garage, in case you get cabin fever."

"Cabin fever?"

"That means the walls are closing in and you need to get out. Just don't turn off the main roads. You could easily get lost around here. All the roads look the same."

"Why would I want to leave here and ride around?"

"You might get bored or lonely. But there's no need to be afraid. You're safer here than in the city."

"Who could possibly be bored or lonely here?"

She and Sammy stood on the edge of the yard watching Zack's car move down the mountain and out of sight.

Two hours after he left, she understood bored and lonely. Loneliness crept in with the fog, and everything was boring. She found herself wanting Zack to call and felt guilty that she had not learned more about him.

She had never seen Zack close the curtains, day or night. He had said there was nothing out there to be afraid of. Alone at night after the sun went down, she pulled all the curtains together and locked the doors and windows. She was not exactly afraid. She felt strange, like someone was watching her.

The day of his return, she was resting on the patio lounger, reading *Gone With The Wind*, and feeling lazy with nothing to do. She heard voices and looked up to see a woman wearing floppy overalls walking up the driveway with one child on her hip, another at her side.

"Hey," the woman said, brushing back her brown, fuzzy hair. "I never been up here b'fore. It's as purty as Minnie said. She told me you got a young 'un Frank's age."

"Good morning. I'm Abby and this is Sammy. I didn't realize anyone lived up here except Oliver and Minnie."

"I don't live up here. I'm from down yonder," the woman said and pointed to the valley. "I knowed it wuz a fur piece, but I didn't think about it being so steep. Whee. I'm plumb tuckered out."

"Come sit," Abby said. "Have a glass of iced tea."

"Don't go to no trouble," the woman said.

"No trouble at all. Glad to have the company."

Abby went in the house to get another glass and returned with several of Sammy's toys. She gave Willard to the baby, a truck to Frank, and a box of Kleenex to the woman to wipe mucus from the youngest boy's nose. Sammy had already made friends with the boys.

"How old are your children?" Abby said.

"They's two and a half and four. Had 'um close together."

"I'm Abby Crowley," she repeated.

"I know who you are. Talk gits around Soda Creek."

"I didn't get your name," Abby said.

"Pro'bly cause I forgot to give it. I'm Nita June Foster and this is Billy and Frank. We live off Ducket Ridge in a trailer. You've pro'bly heard us yelling at night."

"I don't hear much of anything up here but an occasional hoot owl. Sometimes, it's so quiet, it's scary. It's like Heaven. In fact, I've named it *Paradise.*"

"Paradise. That's a likely name for this place. You kin' visit me if you git lonesome. I'm by m'self most days and purt' near ever' Fri'dy and Sad'dy night."

"Does your husband work on those nights?"

"Not 'zac'ly. He more or less plays on them nights."

Abby left well enough alone. It had been a good visit and she was glad to know someone her age in the area.

"Well, I got to go now," Nita June said, and got up.

"How far did you say it was to your place?"

"'Bout two miles."

"You walked two miles? That's too far to carry Billy on your hip and for little Frank to walk. Goodness. He's just a baby. I'll call Minnie and we'll take you home."

After she and Minnie took Nita June home, and Sammy was in bed, she heard Zack's car. He was carrying an armload of gifts when he came through the door.

"Zack, I want you to stop bringing gifts. I can't accept all these things. How long is this going to last?"

"What?"

"Me living here. The gifts."

"You can live here as long as you want to. I think it's customary for people to accept gifts. Besides, you've only been here a couple of weeks."

"You know what I mean. What am I going to do?"

"I'll never tell you what to do, Abby. You'll have to make your own decisions around here."

"I don't know where to start."

"Then don't start. There's plenty of time. Did you go sightseeing?"

"I don't know how to drive."

"I can't imagine anyone this day and age not knowing how to drive." Thinking he might have embarrassed her, he said, "But then, I suppose you didn't need to drive."

"Bob took the bus to work," she said. Saying her husband's name made her feel ashamed and ignorant. Zack was right. It was unusual not knowing how to drive. She didn't know how to do much of anything. Cook, clean, take care of a child and wait on a man. *Yady, yady, yah. No self-pity allowed.*

"I'll teach you to drive so you can go meet the neighbors. You'll have to approach them, though. They pretty much stay to themselves around here."

"Then you'll be surprised to know I had visitors today."

"Who?"

"Nita June Foster and her two sons."

"That's great. You're already making friends."

In her other life, making friends would have caused a fight. Seeing Nita June reminded her of what she'd just as soon forget, and made her realize how fortunate she was to have escaped. "I wonder if the police are hunting me."

"You were defending yourself. That's no crime. The police have no reason to look for you. I doubt that anyone filed a missing person's report, under the circumstance. Why're you thinking about all this? Do you want to call Bob?"

"God, no. I never want to talk to him, nor see him."

"I've got an idea. Let's go to the Gold-Fest."

"What's a Gold-Fest?"

"You'll see," he said.

They drove down in the valley where autumn was spreading a calico blanket across the slopes. Small rental cabins sat off the highway around Soda Creek Village. In the summer, Christian groups and campers came to enjoy mountain recreation, like white water rafting, horseback riding and gold panning. During the Gold Festival weekend, people came from across the country to display their arts and crafts. The locals demonstrated cane grinding, syrup making, basket and chair weaving, gold panning in Soda Creek. Horseback riders fringed the area as frilly dressed cloggers clicked their heels to old time mountain music of fiddles, guitars, banjos, and hammered dulcimers.

Because they would be gone till late in the evening, Oliver agreed to stay with Sammy. The boy helped Oliver in the green house for a while, and then took his trucks to the yard. He was still playing outside at dusk.

When Oliver turned on the floodlights, he heard a rustle in the woods beyond the yard.

"Zelphie? Is that you?" No reply. "May be that old bear." He picked up the toys and took Sammy in the house.

Chapter Six

Zelphie Crabtree leaned her walking stick against a tree and sat on a rock to tie her brogan string. She was tired from toting groceries almost four miles from the store. Peach, her faithful Rottweiler, laid at her feet.

Some people called her crazy for walking through the woods. But the doctor didn't call her crazy. He labeled her with a long medical term she couldn't remember, which meant she was hyperactive. The pills he prescribed made her feel weird, so she threw them in the ditch and used her grandpa's remedy for what he called *warrior fever.* Most everybody thought he was a Cherokee medicine man. Fact be known, he was not Indian at all. He had simply been a curious child and remembered the natural remedies used by adults who were friends with the Indians. At ninety-four, he learned Zelphie had inherited the fever and told her how to handle the disease. "Drink herb tea, lots of spring water, and run, or walk until it goes away."

So, the woods had become familiar to Zelphie. When she was younger, she ran. Now, at eighty-four, she was content to walk.
She had not intended to come this way today. But it was closer and she was tired. By dusk, she was outside the *mansion* on the mountain. The curtains were drawn. Zack was out of town. The city woman was afraid.

She liked Zack. He was a good man. He enjoyed the woods almost as much as she did. Sometimes, if he were outside, she would stop and visit. Most times she would see him sitting at his desk, writing, with a phone to his ear. Or, looking at his computer, the new technology that was ruining the world. The beast that was feeding children's minds with unreal tales and fantasies and keeping them from learning to live with God's nature. They would grow up not knowing how to survive during the Bible's tribulations. Some day, electricity would go off permanently. The new generation would be lost without the beast, dwindle to nothing; go to the devil. That was how the world would end.

Abby had seen the movie *Gone with the Wind.* Now, she had read the book. Scarlett's husbands had been good to her. They had all died, except Rhett. Men were afraid of her feistiness, yet, it was her spunk that made her attractive to them. She wondered how Scarlett would have handled an abusive husband. There was no telling. One thing for sure. Scarlett would not have stayed with an abuser. And, after leaving, Scarlett would not have been idle. She would have done something.

Abby held the book to her chest. *Waiting for the future to handle itself, or sitting around doing nothing, letting Zack take care of everything, will not give me the independence I crave. I must make a move.*

She put the book away and found Zack in his office.

"How do you get a divorce in Tennessee?"

He looked shocked.

Good. I'm going to start shocking lots of people.

"You'll need a lawyer. Why?"

"Just curious. If you don't mind, look into it for me. And give me the name of a good lawyer," she said. "How long will you be gone?"

"Couple of days," he said.

She turned and walked out of his office.

That night she kept thinking about divorce. The Catholic Church was dead-set against it. Good Catholics confessed a lot and stayed married, which often meant living in hell. What they thought didn't matter to her any more. A life without fear, being free—that's what mattered. She was ready to do whatever it took to get it. The first thing she had to do was learn to drive. Then she would find a means of support.

Loud noises of a raving maniac rang from inside the trailer on Ducket Ridge. Nita June took the boys to the back room and locked herself in with them. Years of watching the same scene had taught her to remove herself and the boys from his presence. It was the only solution. Reasoning with him was out of the question when he was in a drunken state. She didn't know how or where he got whiskey in a dry county. Having lived in the area all his life he probably belonged to a moonshiner's secret club of bootleggers and users. If she had a phone in the bedroom, she'd call Zelphie. Though most people didn't pay much mind to the old woman, she made perfect sense to Nita June. Last winter when doctor's bills were mounting and Billy was getting no better, the old woman's remedies cured his bronchitis and sore throat.

The racket finally stopped. Nita June slowly sneaked down the hall to the living room where her husband lay passed out on the couch. She lit a cigarette and sat looking out the window where the new moon illuminated the woods almost like it was day. A shadow moved in the bushes. She propped her head on her hand and said, "Thank You, Sweet Jesus."

Sammy had been rambunctious all day. Abby was relieved when he finally went to sleep. Shortly after she finished the laundry, Zack came home.

He was quieter than usual. She tried to think of something that would provoke a conversation with him.

"Do you ever use these guns?"

His eyes sparkled as he eagerly took the guns from the case. Two of them had belonged to his parents.

"Your mother had a gun?"

"She was an excellent shot."

"Where are your parents?"

"They're gone," he said in a whisper, took a deep breath and then changed the subject. "Guns are as dangerous or as safe as the person using them. Always keep the case closed and locked so Sammy can't get it open."

"I doubt that I'll be opening the case, Zack. Sammy can't even reach it."

"My friend gave me this one while we were in Africa. The friend in France, with the son. And this one is light enough for you. Here. Feel it. I'll teach you to shoot tomorrow after you learn to drive."

"Why should I learn to shoot? I don't want to kill anything. You said it was safer here than in the city."

He put away the guns and said, "Maybe you'll never have to shoot, but it's good to know how, if you need to. I got so carried away with the guns I almost forgot the news. I spoke to Charlie Donelson, my attorney friend in Addisonville. He says your divorce will be simple. You have an appointment with him next Wednesday."

"Do you trust him?"

"Above anyone else. I consult him on everything."

"Somehow, I thought getting a divorce would be hard," she said. "You seem troubled. Are you okay?"

"I had a rough day. That's all."

"Me too."

"What happened here?"

"Nothing, really," she said. It was just like him to divert the conversation, talk about others instead of himself. "For one thing, Sammy was restless. Minnie took us to see Nita June. I think she has problems."

"Who? Nita June? What kind of problems does she have?"

"I'm not sure. She won't talk about it."

"Can I help?"

"Probably not. She seems unhappy, or trapped." *Like I was.*

"Did you meet her husband?"

"No. He's gone a lot. Maybe that's why she's anxious."

"Or, maybe she was having a bad day, too. That happens to all of us at times for no reason. Why was Sammy restless?"

"I think he had what you call cabin fever. Could be he thought you were coming home. But he was probably just tired. He didn't get grumpy until around bedtime. Wouldn't go sleep till he could no longer hold his eyes open."

"I'll check on him," Zack said.

She followed and watched him brush the blond hair from her son's face, then pull a quilt around his shoulders. A warm feeling stirred inside her. *Zack would make a good father.*

In the middle of the night, long after Abby had gone to sleep, Zack crept out and drove down in the valley to the small church where the doors were always unlocked. He sat on a back seat in the dark, took a small Bible from his pocket and held it in his hand. He didn't need to open it. He knew the passage by heart. Matthew 28:20: *Lo, I am with you always, even unto the end of the world.*

He didn't know what to say and was hoping God would read his mind. *You're the Father. I'm the child. Though I haven't been a very good child lately. I need Your help. I'm up against something I just don't think I can handle alone.*

The door of the church slowly opened and a woman came in and sat down about half way to the front. Moonlight from the window wasn't bright enough for Zack to recognize her. *Does she need help? Maybe I should approach her. Remember where you are, Zack. Didn't you come for help?*

He put the Bible in his pocket and sneaked out trying not to disturb whoever it was.

Zelphie pulled her jacket together and sat still. *What possible problem could Soda Creek's richest man have?*

Zack and Oliver built a sand bed with low rails around the sides so Sammy could climb in and out. Even in late October the weather was warm enough for him to play outside. Harvey, the white horse sat beside him in the sand. Willard, the monkey sat on the chest of drawers in the bedroom.

After lunch, Abby and Sammy put away his toys and walked to the lake. By the time they returned Zack had finished working in his office. They all went down in the valley for Abby's first driving lesson. It was easier than riding a bike. She loved it and wanted to drive home up the steep road.

"Let's stick to flat land for a while. Driving up the steep road can be frightening if you look over the side of the cliff. Anyway, it's time for you to learn to shoot."

That, too, seemed natural for Abby.

"You learn fast. You're a better shot than I am. But something's on your mind. You seem a little distracted."

"I'm sorry, Zack. Guns make me nervous."

"It's more than that."

"Maybe I'd like to know more about the man who has so graciously turned over his home to me and my son."

"Like what?"

"Where you were born. Where you work. Anything."

"I was born in Texas. I work wherever I am," he said. "How about grilled burgers for supper?"

She put her nose in the air and went inside. *Why does he always avoid personal questions?*

She had never thought of herself as the out-door type. Yet, she woke up at the crack of dawn, eager to follow Zack down trails in every direction around his house. The more she explored and listened to the sounds of nature, the more she relaxed and felt at ease. This truly was *Paradise.* She had fallen in love with the Tennessee mountains and the Soda Creek community. Though Zack was never gone more than two nights a week, she found herself dreading to be alone.

"Don't you get tired of traveling?"

"Sometimes. More now than ever," he said and turned to Sammy. "Promise to be a good boy and I'll bring a surprise."

"I promise."

"When you get back I'd like to talk to you about finding a job," she said as he put his briefcase in the car.

"We can fix that right now. What kind of work experience do you have?"

"Not much."

"Do you know anything about office work? Computers?"

"I can type, file, make appointments and have basic computer knowledge. I've operated the computer at the library."

"Good. Do the filing. Turn off the answering machine. Take my calls. Get acquainted with the computer." He wrote on the back of a card. "This is the computer password. And," he said, pulling out his wallet, "here's an advance on your salary. I've got to run or I'll miss my flight."

She stood holding five hundred dollars in her hand as he drove away. She didn't know whether to be mad or glad.

As if he needs office help. This is just more charity. So? What's wrong with that? Now, he's my boss, that's what. Well, sort of. More like a good brother. Don't know. Never had one. If I did, I'd want one like Zack. But I really don't want a brother. They come and go as they please, don't tell you what they do, where they go, who they see. Maybe Zack has a girlfriend. Maybe he's gay. He certainly hasn't shown intimate feelings for me. He's so secretive. Having secrets is no sin. Living in his house is no sin. I know sin. Life before Zack. Controlled by a drunken idiot. That was sin. Forget any religion saying that wasn't sin.

The filing was easy. She turned on the computer, played solitaire and surfed the net. She would need another password to open Zack's private files. She propped her feet on the desk. *So this is office work. Piece 'o cake. Training for the future.*

She was too restless with excitement to sleep. Remembering Zack had mentioned a highchair in the attic, she decided to see what else was up there. She went up the stairs and opened the door. Attics were supposed to be junky. Not here. Odds and ends on the shelves lining each side of the attic were neatly organized like the rest of the house. There was the highchair he mentioned. A crib. A box of toys. Along the end of the attic were four closed doors. She opened one and froze. She quickly opened another. Then another. Closets. Filled with women's designer clothes and shoes. They must have cost a fortune. Probably his mother's. Why would he keep them?

It was midnight when she finally went to bed. Sleep wouldn't come. Her head was filled with questions. What was he hiding? She wondered if the attic held the answer.

Chapter Seven

Getting a driver's license was easy. At first she drove straight to town and back every day, staying on the main road like Zack said. *Obey. Obey.* Driving thrilled her more than anything she could remember. It gave her confidence, made her feel bold enough to turn off on a side road one day. Curve after curve she drove until the road became narrow, like a wagon trail she had seen in a western movie. The woods got thicker. The ditches disappeared. There were no houses. No side roads. She became frantic and stopped, almost in tears.

"It's pretty out here in the woods, Mommy," Sammy said.

"What a brave little man you are."

She looked up and saw a man standing in front of the car. He was holding a shotgun and three dogs on leashes. Her shaking fingers pushed the button to lock all the car doors.

He approached, bent down and looked through the window.

"What ya'll doin' way back in heah?"

"I took a wrong turn," she yelled through the window. "Where does this road lead?"

"It don't lead nowhere. It ends after a piece up ahead. Ya'll haf'ta turn around and go back how ya' come."

"Thank you," she said, found a place to turn around and retraced her route until she found Highway 68.

"Well," she said to Sammy. "That wasn't so bad."

Since she had to pass Ducket Ridge on the way home, she visited Nita June and spilled the adventure.

"I'm telling you I've never been so scared in my life."

"Sounds like one o' them old Marlin men. They hunt back in there a lot. They wouldn't hurt a human," Nita June said.

"Well, that's good to know. Next time I wander on side roads, I'll come get you."

"I'd like that very much."

After a short visit, Abby headed home feeling brave and independent. Sitting at Zack's desk, she dialed her old Chicago number. *I won't tell Bob to go where the sun doesn't shine. I'll hang up without saying a word. This time, I'm in control.*

The phone was disconnected. She dialed information. Bob's name was not listed. *So much for my great detective work.*

She sorted Zack's mail, filed reports and typed memos. Then she plundered, looking for anything personal. *Am I nosey? No. Just curious.*

She jumped when the phone rang.

"This is Mrs. Williams, Dear. I need to speak with Zack."

"He's not in at the moment. May I take a message?"

"It's very personal. But, it's most urgent. Can you get a message to him immediately?"

"Certainly," Abby said, though she had no way of knowing how to reach him immediately, or later.

"Tell him I said it's time. Thank you, Dear."

Strange message. Urgent message. Deliver it. How?

Did he say where he was going? She knew he worked for CCI. According to information she found on his desk, they had offices in Denver, Chicago, Atlanta and Dallas. She dialed Denver.

"CCI. May I help you?"

"I need to speak with Zack Cole."

"Who's calling, please?"

"I, ah . . .."

"Hello? Anybody there?"

She hung up.

Who's calling? His home secretary. The one who's living with him. Dumb. In his house? Yeah. His girlfriend? No!

49

She planned her strategy more carefully and dialed Chicago.

"May I speak to Zack Cole, please?"

"Who shall I say is calling?"

"This is Abby, his home office secretary," she said firmly.

After a pause, the voice said, "One moment please."

Shortly, the voice said, "I'm sorry. Mr. Cole is not in the Chicago office today. May I take a message?"

"Tell him to call home as soon as possible," Abby said. She left the same message in Atlanta and would call Dallas after Sammy's snack. The call was delayed by Oliver's visit.

Good. He'll know where to find Zack. What will I say? Where is the man I've been living with for over a month?

"Do you know how I can reach Zack?" she said.

"Is something wrong?"

"It's personal, Oliver. I want to give him a message."

She hated being mean to Oliver. She hated feeling helpless more. *It's like I've been kidnapped. That's stupid. I came willingly. Never thought of it, but I can't do anything without Zack's help. I can do nothing. Nothing. Always depending on men. No use asking Oliver. He's a man. He won't talk about Zack. He'll insist that we go off on some God-awful Indian trail so he can spin more tales.*

She told Oliver she had a headache and sent Sammy for an ice cream.

She called Dallas.

"I must speak with Mr. Cole immediately."

"May I ask who's calling?"

"This is Mrs. Crowley at his home office. Mr. Cole is in the Dallas office today, is he not?"

"Yes. I'll take your number . . . ."

"I need to speak to him now," Abby cut in.

"He's in a meeting. He'll have to call you back."

"What's your name?" Abby said, firmly.

"Sherry."

"Sherry. I'd hate to tell Mr. Cole that you're responsible for him not getting this most urgent message."

"I'll see if he can take the call."

Abby held the phone to her ear, feeling like the queen of Sheba, a bossy bitch, or somebody like that.

"Zack Cole."

"Zack, this is Abby."

"Sorry, what was that name again?"

She could almost see him smiling.

"You know who this is."

"Ah, yes. Mrs. Crowley. What's the problem?"

"You had an urgent call from Mrs. Williams. She said to tell you it's time."

His silence was scary.

"Zack. Did you hear me?"

"Yes, of course. I'm in a meeting at the moment. I will handle that when I get home *tonight*. Thanks for calling, Mrs. Crowley," he said and hung up.

She held the phone several seconds before she put it on the receiver. Her enthusiasm was gone. Maybe he had acted weird because she had interrupted an important meeting. How stupid. Her first week on the job and he would probably fire her tonight when he got home. He did say tonight, didn't he? She hated to face him.

She called the airline Zack used. They wouldn't say if he was on their flights. But they gave Abby the arrival time for the next three flights from Dallas to Knoxville.

After putting Sammy to bed, Abby sat in the plush chair beside the window and waited. The ticking of the clock above the fireplace got louder and slower and almost lulled her to sleep. She saw a flicker of light in the woods. Squinting, she saw it again. Something moved out there. Must be an animal. She got up, locked the doors and pulled the drapes.

By 2:00 a.m. she had drank a pot of coffee to stay awake. Needing something to calm her nerves, she found the wine in the pantry. Her knowledge of wine was zero. Pink was pretty. She opened a bottle of blush and filled her glass. It tasted fruity and sweet. After one glass she felt good. After two, she felt even better. *How will I justify my actions? The message was urgent. Mrs. Williams said so.* Soon she was relaxed, not concerned with anybody's actions. She woke up as Zack opened the front door and put his briefcase on the table beside the window.

"I'm sorry I was short with you on the phone," he said.

"What?" She was stunned, dizzy and sick in her stomach.

He picked up the empty wine bottle. "Abby. Did you drink the whole bottle?" He laughed, shook his head. "I didn't realize you drank wine. You never cease to amaze me."

He never ceased to amaze her. "You're not mad at me?"

"I could never be mad at you. None of this is your fault. I left you completely in the dark. If you're going to take care of my office, you should know how to reach me. It's time you knew about my personal affairs. I've wanted to tell you. I just didn't know how."

"I don't need to know your personal affairs to work in your office. I don't need to know anything about you to live in your house." Shocked at her own voice, she put her hand over her mouth. *My words are slurry and stupid.*

"You need to hear this and I need to say it. The only way I know to tell you is to blurt it out. I'm married."

That got her attention.

"Married? Oh, my God. Does your wife know I'm living with you? I mean, here? In your house?"

"Let me explain," he said.

"There's nothing to explain. You're married. I'm married. The whole darn world is married. Why did you bring me here? What are you doing, Zack? Never mind. I'll leave tomorrow."

"You're not going anywhere until I explain. I know it's the oldest line in the book, but I fell for it and I'm telling you whether you want to hear it or not. I thought my wife was pregnant when we got married. I didn't love her, but I didn't want my child raised without a father. When it was obvious there would be no child, I confronted her and she left in a rage. Her car slid over the cliff as she sped down the mountain. She's been in a coma for three years."

"God. I don't know what to say. This is so awful."

She wanted to comfort him, say everything was all right. But, it wasn't. She rubbed her brow, unable to think straight. Why did she drink the stupid wine? She was feeling dizzy, wanting to puke, needing to sleep.

Zack stood looking out the window where dawn was starting to cast its red glow over the mountains.

"I should have told you a long time ago. But you were in trouble. I knew if I told you my problems you wouldn't accept my help."

"And, by helping me you've made a bad situation worse. My head is hurting so bad I can't think straight. I can't even talk right. I'm going to bed. We'll talk in the morning."

"It's already morning, Abby."

"Whatever." She threw her hands in the air. "I hope you called Mrs. Williams. She said it was urgent."

"That's what this is about. Let me finish."

"No. I can't stand to hear anymore of this horrible story," she said and went to bed.

She woke up feeling like she had been run over by a steamroller. She was confused, tired, and felt like her head would explode any minute. *Did Zack say he had a wife in a coma?* She rushed to the window and looked in the garage. The Ferrari was gone. Why would he leave at a time like this? She would never understand him. Was he visiting Oliver? Not in the Ferrari. She started back to the kitchen and saw a note by the phone.

Sammy is with Minnie and Oliver. Please forgive me. I'll be back tonight. I can be reached at the numbers on the desk. Call if you need me. Love, Zack.

If I need him? She needed to talk, but not to him. She dialed Nita June's number. No answer. She called Minnie and within minutes, Oliver's truck was outside.

Just like you Minnie. Send the equalizer. The terminator. The controller. A man.

"Come on in, Oliver. Where's Minnie?"

"She thought I should come while she keeps Sammy. Zack told

me what happened. I've never seen him torn up like this."

"Nice of him to tell you *my business*. Why won't he talk about his parents?"

"When Zack's father learned Zack's mother had an incurable disease, he sold everything he owned. They traveled everywhere together. Strange how Mr. Cole prayed they'd go together. And they did. He was piloting Zack's small plane when it crashed. Took both at once, almost like he'd planned it."

"That's so sad. Zack's whole life is sad, yet he hides it so well. Does Zack have sisters or brothers?"

"Not that I know of."

"Did he think I was so shallow I wouldn't understand about his wife being in a coma?"

"Would you be here now if you had known he was married?"

"Maybe. If he'd told me the whole story. He's the best friend I've ever had, Oliver. I'm hurt that he didn't confide in me. Look how he has helped Sammy and me. I want to help him. What can I do?"

"The best thing to do is let him work it out."

"What kind of business is CCI?"

"It'd be hard to say. Computers, oil, airplanes."

"I'm so mad. Everybody in Soda Creek probably knows."

"No. They don't. Zack keeps his affairs to himself."

"I can vouch for that. I guess I'm more mad at myself. If I hadn't been so selfish he might have confided in me."

"Zack's a master at solving problems. It may take a while, but he'll work it out." He got up and patted her shoulder. "Why don't you come visit with me and Minnie today?"

"Maybe later this afternoon."

"Its already afternoon."

"Then, I'll go tomorrow. I have to think."

"We'll keep Sammy for a while, if you don't mind."

"That's probably a good idea."

The hospital room was familiar to Zack. Lines moved across

monitors hooked to a body lying still on the bed, with white sheets pulled up under her arms. Her long black hair had been brushed and pulled around on her chest.

"Mrs. Williams says there's a change for the worse."

"I'm sorry, Zack. There's nothing more we can do," the doctor said.

Zack stood alone, looking at the body on the bed.

Maybe things would have been different if you had been pregnant. But, could even a child make a loveless marriage of deceit successful? Probably not.

Lately it seemed like an unknown force was controlling his life. And, it was okay. He no longer had a burning desire to kill all the evil in the world. He was seeing good in all things. A reason for everything. Guilt had made him keep Marie alive with machines, always thinking he caused it. That no longer made sense. Standing by the woman who had deceived him in every way, he realized he had done to Abby what he disliked about Marie.

The pregnancy conspiracy was not her only deceptive act. He had given up trying to unravel her lies long ago.

The nurse opened the door and said, "Mrs. Williams and her daughter are outside with a priest. Shall I bring them in?"

"Of course. Bring them in."

"Hello, Zack," Mrs. Williams said, placing her hand on his.

"This is the hardest thing I've ever had to do. Are you sure . . .?" Zack's words trailed off.

"Mother and I have been sure for a long time," Cilia said. She walked to the bed and touched her sister's hair. "We were waiting for you to make up your mind, Zack."

"My dear son-in-law. It's time we stopped playing God."

With the doctor, nurse and minister standing by, Zack reached for the switch. Tears swelled in his eyes. He pulled back his hand, looked at his mother-in-law and said, "I'll always take care of you."

"You've already done more than was necessary. Marie has been gone for a long time. You must move on with your life and find happiness."

She hugged him briefly, then took his hand and placed it on the switch. Pressing her hand on his, together they turned off the life support.

Chapter Eight

Abby sat by the window watching the sun creep over the mountains casting its peach trim around the dark blue sky. She had slept well and was ready to greet Zack. While going through his own kind of misery, he never failed to help others. Like Oliver had said, Zack was a good man. Being so wrapped up in self-pity and confused about her future, she had failed to let him know how she appreciated what he had done for her and Sammy. She had to tell him how wonderful he was. Then, she would once again ask his help in finding somewhere else to live.

She put on gloves and went to the rose garden to select a bouquet for the table. Assorted colors. Or, maybe yellow, for forgiveness. Which color means friendship? Suddenly, the beauty of the white Meidilands touched her. The decision was made. White for purity, perhaps a fresh start.

Zack walked in as she was placing the bouquet on the table.

His face was sad and rugged. Without a word, she opened her arms, to which he came, trembling, trying to hold back tears.

"What is it? Please tell me. No more secrets between us."

He looked into hers eyes and said, "God, I hope I've done the right thing. I am so sorry for everything."

He cupped her face in his hands, then moved them slowly around her neck beneath her silky hair.

"Can we eat now? I'm hungry." Sammy stood in the doorway, clinging to Harvey.

Zack wiped his eyes and picked up Sammy. "Just what does your tummy call for this morning, young man? Shall I whip up one of my special omelets?"

"Yeah. A big one."

"I think that can be arranged," Zack said.

"Let me cook this time," Abby said.

"No. I need to do this."

"I'm beginning to think you don't like my cooking, Mr. Cole," she said.

Zack's eyes rolled back. It was good to see him smile.

After breakfast, Sammy gathered his trucks in front of the fireplace.

"I want to apologize," he said as they cleared the table.

"You don't owe me an apology, nor an explanation," she said and closed the dishwasher.

"Sit down, please. I want to tell you everything."

He explained Marie's lies about her family, and the visit to the hospital where he finally laid his guilt to rest with help from Marie's mother and sister.

"Mrs. Williams told me not to let myself inflicted guilt get in the way my happiness, which is exactly what I was doing. Only then did I realize I had to let go of the past, which in itself was distorted. The past and future had to be separated."

"Then . . . she's gone?"

"Yes," he said.

"I'm sorry, Zack. I really am."

"I wanted to tell you in person. There is so much I want to say to you, Abby. . . . " The phone rang. "I'll be right back." He ran upstairs to his office. In a few minutes, he came down with a frown on his face.

"I have to leave again. I'll be in Dallas if you need me. There will be no more secrets. I owe you that much."

"You owe me nothing, Zack. It is I who will forever be indebted to you."

With Peach beside her, Zelphie Crabtree walked in the cool, night rain. She paused outside Nita June's trailer. Above the sound of the rain on the trailer's roof, she heard a child's whimper. Moving closer, she found Frank, crouched behind a bush. Blood on his lip was mixed with rain and tears. She pulled him close, holding him under her long slicker.

"There's a cold spell moving in tonight. You'd better come home with Ole Zelphie," she said, and led the boy through the woods to her cabin.

Inside the trailer, clothes were strung, tables were turned over, lamps and dishes were broken on the floor. At a quarter past midnight, Nita June grabbed the ringing phone so it would not awaken her drunken husband.

"Hello," she whispered.

"Frank is with me."

"Oh, my God. I thought he wuz in his room."

"He's safe." The phone went dead.

Abby was sipping her first cup of coffee when Nita June knocked on the door.

"Come in. Want some coffee, or juice?" Abby said.

"One cup of coffee. Then, I gotta go get Frank."

"Get him from where?" Abby poured coffee for Nita June and juice for Billy. Sammy ran to his bedroom and returned with Willard. Billy grabbed the monkey by the tail and said, "Mine."

"He stayed at a friend's house last night."

"Just a friendly sleep-over?"

"You might say he spent the night with his Guardian Angel."

"That's a good place to spend the night." She didn't want to be nosy, but when Nita June offered no explanation, she said, "Are you sure you won't stay for a while?"

"Naw. I really have to go,"

"Nita June, I'm going to tell you something I have told no one else. It will stay between us."

Nita June poured herself more coffee and listened without speaking as Abby told about her life before Zack brought her to Soda Creek. She had hoped Nita June would talk about her life, but she didn't. She made no comment about anything Abby said. At least, she knew someone understood.

After they left, Abby and Sammy took their daily walk to the lake, before Sammy settled in the sand bed.

"I'm going in for a minute. Don't leave the yard."

Before she reached Zack's office, Sammy screamed. She ran out and saw a snake in the sand bed. She grabbed Sammy from the back. The snake struck at her, but missed. With Sammy in the house, she grabbed a shotgun from the case, filled it with buckshot and ran outside. Boom, she fired. The snake's head was gone. Its tail flopped and wiggled.

She was shaking so, she could hardly put the gun away. Sammy was still screaming his head off.

Oliver's truck pulled up. She ran to the door and yelled, "It's okay, Oliver. I just killed a snake."

"I see. A copperhead. Did it bite you?"

"No. It was in the sand bed with Sammy."

Oliver immediately examined the boy. "The snake bit Sammy on the arm. Get in the truck."

He took a handkerchief from his neck, tied it above the bite marks, cut an x with his knife, then sucked the blood from the bite while Sammy screamed. He slid under the wheel, sped down the mountain, around the curvy roads toward the nearest hospital, forty-five minutes away.

Abby sat in the waiting room, looking beyond the shiny floors to the double doors where they had taken Sammy. At 10:30 p.m., she rushed to a nurse who came through the doors.

"Is my son okay?"

"The doctor will speak to you in a minute," the nurse said and went down the hall.

"Of course, he's okay," Oliver said. "Children's bodies fight poisons better than ours. You're getting to be a real sharp shooter. That snake's head was blown off."

"I shouldn't have come to this place. Living in the woods with snakes and wild animals is just plain backwards. I should have stayed in Chicago."

"Don't say that." Oliver's voice was soothing, almost a whisper. "Sammy loves it here. And, you do, too."

"I shouldn't have let him play outside alone."

"Now, don't go blaming yourself. You couldn't have known."

"I don't want to live if anything happens to Sammy. He's all I've got, all I've ever had."

"Abby, you're just upset. You've got Zack. And you've got Minnie and me. Why, everybody in Soda Creek loves you. But, you've still got Sammy. He'll be okay. How about some more coffee?" he said, fumbling with his change.

"I just can't make good decisions. Nothing I do turns out right," she said, sitting on the edge of the orange vinyl chair, legs crossed, top foot swinging, her eyes fixed on the doors at the end of the hall.

Oliver realized his words were falling on ears that were turned off to the world. Her mood was frightening. Zack had to be notified. How could he explain? He was supposed to be taking care of them.

The doors opened and the doctor came out in green hospital clothing. His face was bleak. With Oliver behind her, Abby jumped up and ran to the doctor.

"Sammy's dead," she said.

"I'm sorry . . .."

Life drained from her body. She turned and walked away. Her head and heart were so empty she didn't hear the doctor finish his sentence, "…it took so long." Nor did she hear Oliver calling after her, "Abby. Wait. Sammy's okay. I'll catch up to you later."

She walked out into the cool, night, mountain air, not knowing, nor caring where she was going. She didn't notice when the darkness of the forest replaced the city lights. *How can I be alive and feel so numb? My son is gone and I don't want to be alive. I want to be dead.*

Oliver paced the floor by the only public telephone in the hospital, while a woman talked endlessly. Finally, he stood next to the phone, arms folded across his chest, staring at the woman until she hung up. He immediately took the phone and dialed Zack's cell phone number.

"Thank God, I reached you. You've got to come home."

"What's the problem?"

"It's little Sammy. He's in the hospital. And Abby's gone and I can't find her."

"Back up," Zack said. "Why is Sammy in the hospital?"

"A Copperhead got in the sand box and bit him on his arm in a vein. But the doctor says he'll pull through."

"And, where's Abby?"

"Well," he stammered, "she thought Sammy was dead. After I heard the doctor's report, I visited Sammy so he'd know I was there. Then, I got in my truck and cruised the hospital area. She was nowhere in sight. I can't find her."

"When I hang up, call the sheriff's office and tell Thad Maloney everything you've just told me. Stay with Sammy. I'll be on the next flight."

Oliver hung up and called the sheriff's office.

"Let me talk to Thad Maloney. It's an emergency."

"The Sheriff won't be here until tomorrow morning."

"Zack Cole said for me to talk to Thad Maloney."

"Cole? The guy from Soda Creek? Why didn't he call?"

"He's out of town. Can I please speak to the sheriff?"

"The sheriff ain't here. Can I help you?"

"Are you a deputy?"

"Yes."

"Well, I guess I can tell you. The young lady staying at Mr. Cole's house is missing."

"Is she from out of town?"

"What difference does that make?"

"How long has she been missing?"

"I'd say, maybe an hour. She was here at the Clearwater hospital, went out for some air and hasn't come back."

"She has to be missing 24 hours before we can start looking for her."

"You need to look now. She couldn't have gone far."

"She'll probably turn up in a little while. Probably just went for a walk."

"I know she went for a walk. She didn't come back."

"Come in tomorrow morning and we'll file a missing person's report," the deputy said and hung up.

"Who was that?" the other deputy said.

"Somebody wanting us to look for a woman who's been gone for an hour."

Chapter Nine

Friday night, after a long week at the factory, Jess, Arty, Nick, and Larry were riding the road with music blaring on the car radio. Larry wondered why he always let them talk him into coming along. He was supposed to be the designated driver since he was the only one who didn't drink. Tonight Jess had the wheel. By midnight, a heavy fog had rolled in making it almost impossible to see the road ahead.

"Your wife's gonna kill you if you don't git home soon," Nick said to Jess.

"I got a right to some fun, workin' like I do all week. If she gives me a ration, I'll give her a taste of what for. It'll all be over by daylight," Jess said, swerving to miss something beside the road.

"What was that?" Larry said from the front passenger seat.

"Must 'a been a deer," Arty said.

"That weren't no deer," Larry said.

"Whatever it wuz, Jess nearly hit it," Arty said.

"It looked like a girl to me," Nick said.

"Pro'bly the ghost woman walking these hills," Larry said.

"I'm gonna prove to you once and for all it ain't no ghost woman," Jess said, wheeled the car around, headed back through the dense fog. The headlights flashed on a woman walking beside the road. He swung the car around and crept along behind her.

"Don't mess with her. She'll put a spell on us."

"Will you hush? Ghosts don't wear tight jeans. I swear, I don't know why we bring you along, Larry," Jess said.

"I was born n' raised in these mountains and I ain't about to ignore a tale I heard from my grandpa and mama," Larry said.

"It's all a bunch o' bull," Jess said. He pulled up beside the woman, leaned out the window. "Hey, purdy lil' thang. You lost? Whur ya goin? Arty, git out and help this gal, if you ain't too scared like Larry."

"I ain't scared a' no woman, night or day," Arty said, opened the back door of the car, got out and walked with the woman. He shined a flashlight in her face, up and down her body, while Jess eased the car along. "Hey! Girl. You crazy or what? Jess, she acts like she don't know we're here."

"Git out and help him git her in the car, Nick," Jess said.

Nick got out of the back seat, then stuck his head back in the window. "You want her up here with you?"

"Naw, stupid. Put her in the back seat," Jess said.

"We taking her to the police, or the hospital?"

"Now that's a stupid question, Larry. We're taking her with us," Jess said.

Arty and Nick laughed.

"Shut up ya' laughing and git her in the car," Jess said.

Arty grabbed her arm. She jerked away.

Jess yelled out the window. "Do I have to tell you two idiots how to do ever'thang? Nick, git a hold o' one arm. Arty, you git the other. Surely both of you kin handle a small girl. I swear. I think this sweet thang needs some tending."

She went limp, like a rag doll. It took both of them to lift her into the back seat.

"Nick. Git up here and take the wheel," Jess said. "I'm gittin' back there with her."

"I'll drive," Larry said.

"You drive too dang slow," Jess said.

Nick raced the car through the fog on Highway 68 south. He slowed to the speed limit as he passed through High Plains on the outskirts of the Cherokee National Forest. Then, he picked up speed, slinging his passengers as he drove further into the mountains on curvy, narrow roads.

While the others passed around a bottle of rut-gut whiskey, Larry sat quiet in the front passenger seat. *This ain't right. Tonight's turning awful. Somebody's gonna get hurt.*

"Pull up here in this roadside park," Jess said.

They lifted the limp, rag-doll woman from the car, laid her on the damp pine straw and mulch.

"This ain't right, man. Look at her eyes. She's in a trance or something," Larry said, pacing back and forth near the edge of the thicket. "I hate what you're doing. We ought to be taking her to the hospital."

"Larry's right," Nick said. "Somethin's wrong with her."

"Course there's something wrong with her. She had a fight with her man. Didn't ya' girlie? Crap. This zipper's stuck."

"Naw, Jess," Arty said. "I mean, somethin' ain't right. She's acting weird. Know how her eyes were all glazed over? Well, they're shut now, like she's dead or somethin'."

"Yeah, Jess. Somethin's wrong. There's blood," Nick said.

"Ain't nothing but a little scratch where I slapped her, trying to wake her up. She's tough. She's got a kid, you idiots," Jess said.

"My God. Do you know her?" Larry said.

Jess lit a cigarette.

"I'm glad I didn't do nothin'," Larry said. "Listen. Hear that? Somethin's movin' out there in the bushes."

"Pro'bly your ghost," Jess said, but nobody laughed.

"Could be a black bear," Nick said.

"We better git out a here," Arty said.

"And jus' leave her?" Larry said.

"Naw, stupid. We're gonna let you take her to the sheriff and tell him how you roughed her up," Jess said.

"I ain't touched her," Larry said.

"Let's go. Somebody'll find her," Jess said, throwing down his cigarette, crushing it with his foot.

"I sure do hate to leave her like this," Larry said.

"If you're so worried, you stay with her," Nick said.

"Yeah. According to your tales, the ghost and goblins are watching. Let them look after her," Arty said.

"Git in the car. Larry, you drive," Jess said.

"That's the first sensible thing you've said all night since ya'll are drunker than the devil," Larry said, slid under the wheel and left heavy skid marks as he drove away. *Maybe I'll come back and check on her later.*

The fog was slowly lifting as the wind picked up. She lay shivering on the damp mulch. A gentle hand rubbed her arm. Something wet and rough wiped her face. A warm, hairy animal laid down beside her. She could feel its breath. She briefly opened her eyes. There was a shadow. Then it was gone. Through the tops of tall trees, the moon was trying to peek from behind clouds rushing across the sky. Like a light going off, the world turned black.

Jack pulled his eighteen-wheeler off the road at a roadside park and left the diesel engine running while he got out to stretch his legs. The truck had been hard to handle in the heavy fog on the dark mountain roads. With the fog lifting and hardly any traffic he should be in Atlanta before noon.

He saw something in the edge of the woods. He ran back to the truck, grabbed a flashlight and moved closer.

"Lord have mercy," he said, shining the light on the body. "Bill. Get over here. Quick," he yelled, stripped off his top shirt and covered the woman. "Ma'am, can you hear me?"

Bill climbed from his resting place behind the seat. "This better be important, waking me from the first sleep I've had in 36 hours," he said as he approached Jack. "What in the world? Is she alive?"

"Just barely. She's soaking wet and the wind's picking up. Get the blanket from the cab and cover her while I try to contact the police."

He rushed to the truck and engaged the CB radio and put it on the police channel.

"Breaker, come on. Anybody read me? I need help."

"Yeah. I read you," a voice said above the squelch.

"Is this the sheriff's office?"

"Naw. This is the High Plains Police Department. What's on your mind?"

"We've got a woman down here. Looks like she's in pretty bad shape. Who am I talking to?"

"Deputy O'Dell. What you mean, you've got a woman?"

"Me and my partner pulled our rig off the road to stretch our legs and found a female in the edge of the woods."

"You say she's in bad shape?"

"Her clothes are torn and she may have been molested, or something. Her eyes are closed, but she's alive."

"Has she been stabbed or shot or anything?"

"Naw. Looks like she's been treated pretty bad, though. I think she needs medical attention."

"What's you're location?"

"Highway 68, five miles north of the Polk county line."

"Can you stay with her till we get there?"

"No way I'd leave her out here like this," Jack said.

"Hang in there, Jack. We're about twenty minutes north, heading your way," O'Dell said and grabbed his keys. "Julie."

"I heard," Deputy Julie Anderson said. "I'll send the ambulance or helicopter."

"Tell 'em I'll be waiting," O'Dell said. "You can come later in the other car."

Monroe County Sheriff Deputy Dorsey had made fresh coffee and opened a box of donuts when the sheriff walked in.

"Want donuts, or just coffee, Sheriff?" Dorsey said. *Something mighty big must be going on to bring the sheriff in two hours early.*

"Coffee's fine," Sheriff Thad Maloney said. "Did you get a call last night about a missing woman?"

"Yeah. A man called. Said a woman walked off from the Clearwater hospital and didn't come back. I told him. . .."

"Is that all the information you got?" Maloney said.

"She weren't exactly missing since she was gone less than an hour when I got the call. It was after midnight. I figured you didn't need to be bothered."

"More like eleven, wasn't it? Next time—no, *anytime* someone's missing, call me regardless of the time."

"The woman was visiting a guy in Soda Creek. I figured maybe she decided to go back where she came from."

"Do you know something about this woman?" Maloney said.

"Well, the guy who called said she was from out of town. Word is, she's living with a man named Cole in the mountains."

"You know better than to listen to the word around here," Maloney said. "People get their tales all tangled up with ghost and convicts. And I don't need your two-cent's-worth about a man you know nothing about."

"What I'm saying . . ."

"I know what you're saying," Maloney said, taking the cup of coffee. "Here's what I'm saying. Cole is my friend. A fine man and a good citizen. Did you call the hospital to see if the boy was all right?"

"What boy?"

"The woman's son. Have you called the morgue to see if the woman turned up there?"

"Well, no," Dorsey said. "I was gonna wait 24 hours."

"Do it. Now," the sheriff said.

"You mean handle this like a missing person?"

Maloney gave him a hard look.

"I'll just make those calls now," Dorsey said.

Maloney went in his office, closed the door and dialed the Clearwater police chief's office. "Let me talk to Kirk."

"He won't be in till around nine," a husky, female voice said. "That you Sheriff?"

"It's me, Sarah."

"How ya' doing? Did Mrs. Maloney tell you about the supper next weekend? We're..."

"This is not a social call. I need to talk to Kirk."

"He's probably still in bed." A moment of silence. "I'll see if I can find him," she said, hung up and turned to the deputy sitting at the desk next to her. "He could do his own calling. But, no. He wants me to wake up the grouchiest man in the county. Well, I'll have him know, I don't work for the Sheriff's department…"

"You gonna make the call, or what?" the deputy said.

Within five minutes, the sheriff had explained to Clearwater Police Chief Kirk Hughes about the missing woman.

"Leaving her kid in the hospital for somebody else to look after doesn't sound like a very smart woman. But, given the actions of young people these days, who can tell? Who notified you?" Hughes said.

"Zack Cole. The man she's visiting in Soda Creek.".

Dorsey peeked in the door and said to Maloney, "The kid's okay. Just a snake bite. The woman's not at the morgue."

Maloney waved his hand for Dorsey to close the door.

"Put patrols on the back roads around the hospital. Cover the motel area. Check businesses on both sides of Interstate-75. Let's hope she wasn't picked up by somebody going to New York or Florida."

"Might be better than her heading in the other direction toward the mountains. If she wandered off into the Cherokee National Forest, it'll take dogs and a miracle to find her."

"I know."

Chapter Ten

At 2:00 p.m. Saturday, the staff watched a man get out of a white Ferrari. Without a word, he went in the sheriff's office. Thad shook his hand and closed the door.

"Is that Zack Cole?" Dorsey whispered.

"In the flesh. I hear he has more money than he knows what to do with," Becky said.

"That man wouldn't need money to put his shoes under my bed," Cheryl said. "Is he married?"

"I hear he's got a wife somewhere. She ain't living with him. That's his girlfriend who walked off from the hospital," Becky said, noticing Dorsey taking in every word. "It's a long story. We'll talk over lunch."

"Can I go to lunch with you?" Dorsey said.

"You can go jump in a lake for all we care," Cheryl said.

Thad wasn't sure how to approach his friend. In one sense, the deputy had followed procedure by not running out to look for a woman who had been gone an hour. Not entering the realm of the law, the logical time to look for her was soon after she left the hospital. Zack's face told him this wasn't going to be a pleasant conversation. He decided on the accusatory method.

"You want to tell me why the lady walked off in the middle of the night and left her young'un at the hospital?"

"You want to tell me why you haven't found her? Seems like a small task. She couldn't have gotten far," Zack said.

"We've had patrols out all day," Maloney said.

"Yeah? Well, she's been out there all night."

"I don't understand why Oliver didn't look for her."

"He did. He couldn't find her. That's when he reached out to you. You should have looked for her right after she went missing, Thad, and you know it."

"Can't imagine what would make her just walk off."

"What difference does it make? You should be concerned with finding her," Zack said.

"We're doing all we can. This is a big county, over half of which is untamed mountain land. You got a picture of her?"

"No. She's around thirty, five-four, 110 pounds, blue eyes, long, blond hair. She got a driver's license here in Monroe County two weeks ago. That shouldn't be too hard for you to get your hands on."

"I didn't know that." Maloney gave instructions.to his deputy on the intercom. "I thought I'd wait to call outside help. When S & R gets involved, we lose control."

"Looks to me like you've already lost control. Like I said, she couldn't have gone far. She's probably sitting somewhere in the woods, scared to death."

"Which way do you think she would go?"

"How should I know, Thad? All I know is she's not familiar with this mountainous area and probably couldn't have found my house if she'd tried. As far as I know, she's never been to Clearwater before."

"Is this woman special to you," Maloney said.

"Her name is Abby Crowley and she's very special to me."

"Didn't mean to get personal. Does she have friends around here she would call?"

"If she had called friends in Soda Creek, they would have taken her home. One thing I know for sure. She wouldn't get in the car with a stranger."

"How can you be so sure?" Thad said.

"I just know. You can trust me on that."

"Well, I think somebody picked her up. But, why didn't they take her home, to the hospital, or bring her here, if they were trying to help her?"

"Christ, Thad. You think somebody would pick her up who didn't want to help her?"

"I'm just covering all angles. We'll find her. I've got my best men on it."

"Yeah? Well I'm putting my best man on it, too."

"Anybody I know?"

"Simon Freely. With him on the case, you can forget outside help."

"Yeah. He's the best," Thad said.

Zack walked away without shaking hands, leaving Thad's door open behind him. The office staff was having snacks.

"You got enough donuts? Maybe I should call *Little Debbie, Krispy Kreme, or Dunkin'* and have another truckload brought in. How about some Cinnamon Rolls or cakes? Why don't you call the steak house, have them bring you all dinners at the county's expense, while a woman is lost out there?" He stormed out leaving the staff with their mouths hanging open.

"You heard the man," Maloney said. "Here's her name and description. Get a copy of her driver's license issued here two weeks ago here in Monroe county."

Oliver was sitting by Sammy's bed where he had been all night when Zack walked in.

"How's my boy?"

Sammy lifted his arms and hugged Zack. "I want Mommy."

"She can't come right now. I'm going to stay with you for a while. Okay?"

"Can we go to your house? I want to go to your house."

"Me, too. We're going soon," Zack said.

"The doctor says we can take him home in the morning. Any word on Abby?"

"Nope. Thad's got all kinds of theories, but they haven't done anything. Didn't anybody see her leave?"

"It was pretty quiet around here. Of course, the doctors and nurses saw her before she left. I swear, Zack, I thought she'd be back in a few minutes."

"You did the right thing," Zack said.

"Well, she couldn't have just disappeared into thin air."

"Mommy disappeared into thin air?"

Zack looked at Oliver, then at Sammy. "She's just stepped out. Nothing for you to worry about. Okay?" He looked at Oliver. "Stay here while I take care of the paper work. We'll probably take him home now. Then, I'll get a *real* detective."

The house was full of well meaning neighbors.

"I appreciate this, Minnie. But you've brought enough food to feed half the wild animals in the Cherokee Forest. There was no need for you to go to so much trouble," Zack said.

"It's no trouble to help someone in need, Zack. Have they found Abby?"

"No. They're eating donuts. Now, if you can herd these people out of here, I can get to work."

"What about the boy?"

"He's fine."

"I mean, who'll look after him?"

"He'll be staying with me. You can come in as usual."

"Okay. But, Oliver and I will be glad to take the boy in."

"I appreciate the offer, Minnie. But, he doesn't need taking in. He needs familiar surroundings," Zack said.

"You know better than me what the boy needs," she said.

"And, Minnie. His name is Sammy," he said and thanked everybody for coming as they gathered to leave.

"Can't figure Abby jus' wunderin' off. Let me know if I kin help," Nita June said. "Call me when you know somethin'."

"Thanks, Nita June," Zack said.

With the house quiet and Sammy asleep, Zack went to his office. He dialed Simon Freely and left a message on the answering machine. "This is Zack. It's Saturday, almost midnight. Call me at home. It's urgent."

She lay in bed looking at pale green walls and ceiling. Her body ached all over, inside and out. The needle from an IV pulled against her arm when she tried to get out of bed. She yelled, "Ouch." There was no sound. She sat up and yelled, "Help." Again, "Help me." But it was only her mind screaming. She wasn't making a sound. The world spun and she laid back against the pillows. Where was she?

"Well, hello, young lady. Welcome to the living," the nurse said. She didn't usually work the graveyard shift, but this weekend she was doing a friend a favor. Most times the 11 to 7 shift was boring. Rarely did they get cases as interesting as the lady admitted Saturday morning. Now, Sunday afternoon, she was finally awake. "Are we feeling better today?"

She opened her mouth. Nothing came out.

"Here, Hon. Have a little water," the nurse said. "I'm Norma. Rest a minute. I'll be right back."

Norma returned with a doctor, whose warm, blue eyes leaped out at the woman in bed almost before his face came into view.

"Well, now. You look better. Can you tell us your name and where you live?" the doctor said.

"Don't be shy, Hon," Norma said. "We're going to take good care of you."

The doctor took her hand, felt her pulse, then examined her eyes with a tiny light.

The woman opened her mouth to speak but words refused to come out. She slung her arm, knocked the pitcher of ice water to the floor. She kicked the white sheet back with her feet and jerked the needle from her arm.

Norma pinned her down and picked up a hypodermic needle. The woman fought to pull away.

"Hold off, Norma. She's trying to tell us something," the doctor said, and gently took the young woman's arm. "Can you tell us your name?"

She tried, but couldn't speak.

"Do you know what year this is? Where do you live?"

"Do you know where you are, Hon?" Norma said.

Questions. So many questions. She pointed to the clipboard when Norma handed it to the doctor.

"Here, you can look. We're trying to find out who you are and what happened to you. Can you tell us anything?"

The woman looked at the chart. Name, UNKNOWN. She looked at the doctor, shook her head from side to side, then tried to get out of bed again.

"Please try to stay calm. We're not going to hurt you," the doctor said. "We want to help you."

The woman fought against him and almost fell off the bed.

"Give her the injection, Norma. It's the only thing we can do right now."

Chapter Eleven

Zack hardly closed his eyes during the night laying in the twin bed next to Sammy. At seven-thirty he sneaked out of the room and was cooking pancakes when Sammy came in and asked for his mother. Zack was trying to explain that she had to go away for a while, when the phone rang.

"How long's it been? A couple of years?"

"How soon can you get here?" Zack said.

"What? No hello, Simon, how ya' been, old Buddy?"

"What are you doing right now?" Zack said.

"Right now? Getting my weekly dose of cholesterol, eating a ham and egg and cheese biscuit from Hardees, fixing to watch a ball game I recorded last night while I was on stake out."

"Then, you're on a case."

"Actually, I'm on two cases," Simon said. "A man wants me to find his wife doing hanky-panky. The other's a corporate thing. A guy heisted a few mil and skipped. Why?"

"I need you to find somebody." Zack had tried to get Simon to work for CCI. He was a specialist at tracking lost people, the best P.I. in Tennessee, or in the world for that matter. But Simon would never fit into a structured atmosphere.

"I don't suppose it can wait."

"Afraid not. The sooner you get started, the better."

"Who are you looking for?"

Zack left Sammy eating pancakes at the breakfast bar and went to the other end of the room, out of hearing range. "Her name is Abby Crowley, a friend of mine. Lost somewhere in the mountains and I'm responsible. I brought her and her four-year-old son here."

"Man, you've got big troubles. What happened?"

"Her son was in the hospital, she thought he was dead. She walked away from the hospital around 10:30 or 11:00 Friday night and disappeared into thin air."

"About thirty-four hours. You said disappeared? Any sign of foul play?"

"I don't know. Nobody's been able to find a trace. I'll explain when you get here."

"I'll take the next flight. You picking me up in Knoxville?"

"You'd better drive," Zack said. "It's just four hours from Nashville. Prepare to stay till the job's done."

"I'll be headed your way in fifteen minutes."

Sheriff Thad Maloney walked in his office at one o'clock Sunday afternoon, and said, "Any word on the missing woman?"

"I talked to the Clearwater Police an hour ago. They still haven't found a trace," the deputy said.

Maloney closed his door and called Zack.

"I was wondering if Mrs. Crowley managed to get back home."

"Not hardly, Thad. It's forty miles from the hospital to my house and she was walking last I heard."

"I was just hoping she'd made it home."

"I told you, she wouldn't know how to get here. I've lived here over fifteen years and very few people can find my house."

"I understand, Zack. It would be real easy for a city girl to get turned around in those mountains."

Maloney hung up, sat back, tapped his pencil on the desk and then dialed the High Plains Police Chief's office.

"He's not in today, Sheriff. I think he's at home."

"Thanks, Julie."

He found Joe Cooper at home and explained the situation.

"I thought we'd find her in this side of the county near I-75. But I'm beginning to think she's in your area. Put patrols out, especially on the back mountain roads."

"It doesn't seem likely she'd come this way. You're talking almost forty miles. We may need an extra car. This is a big area," Joe Cooper said.

"Notify the High Plains's merchants. She recently got a driver's license in this county, but she didn't have it with her. I'll fax a description and send a copy of her driver's license as soon as I can. Frankly, Joe, this is embarrassing."

"Why's that? You know her?" Joe said.

"She's a friend of a friend," Maloney said.

"Oh, I see. Did you say she's from Chicago, visiting Zack Cole in Soda Creek?"

"That's what I said, Joe."

"I know Cole. He's a fine man. But if she's visiting, why does she have a driver's license in this county?"

"Don't know the details. Must have been planning to stay."

"If she's new in the area, you may be on to something, Thad. Most locals couldn't find Cole's house without a map. A city slicker could take a wrong turn, get lost in these mountains and stay lost for months. That's probably what happened to her."

"She wasn't driving, Joe. She was on foot."

"Hmm. That makes a big difference. If somebody picked her up, she could've given them the wrong directions, or…"

"Now you're getting the picture," Maloney said.

"Lord have mercy. I'll do what I can from this end."

After stopping at the Clearwater Police Department, the hospital and the sheriff's office, Simon pointed his 1982 blue and white Cadillac south on Highway 68 toward the mountains. When he pulled up, Zack was firing up the grill.

"I figured you'd be here for supper," Zack said, as Simon gave him a bear hug. "You still like steaks well done?"

"You got it."

"Find anything?"

"Not much. They're passing these out." Freely gave Zack a flyer describing Abby.

"I see you've done you homework. Come on in and tell me what you're thinking while I fix a salad," Zack said.

"Seeing this description changed my original theory," Simon said, taking a seat at the breakfast bar.

Zack put plates on the bar. "Let me have it."

"She went missing Friday night. Say a drunk, or maybe several drunks saw a young, pretty woman walking down the road. Ain't no way they'd pass her without trying to give her a lift. She might have gotten in the car."

"She would never get in the car with a stranger. That, I know for a fact."

"Then, he, or they, could've…"

"Forced her," Zack said.

"Something like that. Where's the boy?"

"Name's Sammy. He's in the back room."

"He's staying with you?"

"Yeah. He's a brave little guy, but he's bound to be scared. I'm the only person he knows or trusts. Minnie's chomping at the bits to get her hands on him. I can't leave him. Not now. He keeps looking for his mother."

"I wondered why you weren't looking for Abby. You're as good at tracking as me."

"That's questionable. Maybe in a day or two I'll get Oliver and Minnie to keep him here, in familiar surrounding. But, they'll probably want to take him to their house, which might magnify his confusion."

"You care a great deal for this woman and child, don't you?" Simon said, rubbing his brown beard.

"Yes, I do," Zack said and explained how and why he brought them to Tennessee.

"Boy, this is tragic. But, after three years of watching you carry guilt over what happened to Marie, it's good to see you alive again."

"Well, that's changed, too. I turned off her life support last Friday."

"Jesus, man," Simon said and put his hand on Zack's shoulder. *What is it with you and the women in your life?* "When it rains, it pours. I was on stake out all weekend. I'll need strong coffee before I start out again."

"Your room's ready. You could sleep first."

"It's only eight o'clock. I've got time to canvas this area before I hit the sack. You got a photo of Abby?"

"No. Strange as it may seem, we never took pictures. But, I found this in her purse." He reached in his pocket and pulled out her driver's license.

"This'll work."

"Did Mommy come home?" Sammy said from the doorway.

"Not yet," Zack said.

"I want her to come home."

"I do too, Sammy."

The boy looked cautiously at the stranger sitting at the breakfast bar, and backed away.

"It's okay. This is Simon. He's our friend."

"My name is Sammy. Have you seen my mommy?"

"Hello, Sammy," Simon said.

"I found some rolled-up stuff in here," Zack said, pulling a package from the refrigerator. "Do you know what it is?"

"That's Pillsbury Doughboy cookies," Sammy said.

"I sure am hungry for cookies. Let's have some of these."

Sammy put his hand on his hip. "We gotta cook 'em first."

"Oh. Reckon you can show me how?"

"Sure. I help Mommy all the time. But you'll have to set the timer on the oven. Mommy said I'm not big enough yet."

Sammy pulled each piece of dough carefully and placed it on the cookie sheet.

"I'll work on my trucks till the timer rings." He climbed down from his stool at the bar and went to the other end of the room, got down on all fours and lined up five trucks in a row.

"He likes trucks," Zack said.

"I can tell. What's the name of his trucking company?" Simon said, touched by the boy's attachment to Zack and visa-versa. "Boy, oh boy. I'm not supposed to get emotional about cases. I'd better go. I'll be in touch."

Norma was surprised that she wasn't tired after pulling another graveyard shift. "Anybody checked Unknown lately?"

"When I looked in a little while ago, she was still asleep. She'll never remember who she is, doped up like that," a young nurse said as she pulled on her coat to leave.

"We have to sedate her, Hon," Norma said. "She keeps trying to leave. God knows she's in no shape for that."

"Well, I'm out 'o here," the young nurse said. "You clocking out now, Norma?"

"After I check on Unknown. Sure hope she remembers her name soon," Norma said and headed down the hall. She pushed the door open. The bed was empty. She rushed back to the nurse's station. "Any tests scheduled for Unknown?" she said.

"None that I know of," a nurse at the desk said.

"She's not in her room," Norma said and dialed security.

Nita June couldn't remember when her husband had been so kind. He didn't raise the usual ruckus Saturday night and he hadn't lifted his hand to her all weekend. He had played with the boys on Sunday, even pecked her on the cheek before he left for work Monday morning. She was still in her robe, clearing the breakfast dishes when Zelphie knocked on the back door.

"C'mon in. I'll pour ya' some decaf," Nita June said.

"Everything all right around here?" Zelphie said.

"Better'n usual. You hear 'bout Abby?"

"A little," Zelphie said, wondering how much Nita June knew. She listened while Nita June repeated a story she had heard twenty times over the weekend. *What can I say to this poor woman? What can I say to anybody?* An hour later, she whistled for Peach and left with her heavy burden. She had to do some hard thinking on how to handle the situation.

Chief Joe Cooper had been in his office fifteen minutes when he called the Sheriff.

"Thad. A private dick by the name of Freely was in here last night asking questions about the missing woman."

"That's Cole's man," Maloney said.

"Well, Freely left, then came back in a couple of hours. He and O'Dell got to talking and they may have something. You see, O'Dell was on duty early Saturday morning when the call came in from the truckers."

"What truckers?"

"A couple of truckers found a woman Saturday morning."

"Lord have mercy. Where did this happen?"

"Down at the Polk county line. Says here, they air-lifted her to Knoxville."

"Christ. Did this woman have a name?"

"No I.D. and she was unconscious," Joe said.

"Did O'Dell file the report?"

"Yeah. He compared the dick's picture from Crowley's driver's license to the description you faxed us and said the woman the truckers found could be Crowley. Since they took her to Knoxville, I guess it's out of our hands."

"Knoxville may be out of our jurisdiction. But whoever accosted that woman the truckers found in Monroe county, whether she's Crowley or not, comes under our jurisdiction," Maloney said and hung up. He started to call Zack, then thought better. He wouldn't get Zack's hopes up until he was sure the two women were the same. Simon would keep Zack informed. Right now he needed to talk to O'Dell, look at the report and see if he could find out what happened to *that* woman. Simon's and O'Dell's theory sounded just about right.

Chapter Twelve

Delta was mad, puzzled and hurt. She had been the top computer tech for five years, with more overtime than anybody on the company's record. The job was her life. Working all hours of the night to keep the computers in tip-top shape was more of an enjoyment than a chore.

It all happened after Greta, the new boss from hell, invaded the office with her new regime. Delta went to the office at 1:00 a.m. to repair a computer. She walked in on Greta's little party and was fired on the spot.

Two lawyers said she had a very good chance of winning a lawsuit against Greta. Delta was given no reason for being fired. She also had a copy of the work order, signed by Greta, stating that she could enter the office at anytime, day or night, to repair computers. After worrying about it for a while, Delta decided she didn't need the hassle. She had saved a little money and her car was paid for. Forget Greta's arrogant butt. Let her fix her own stupid computers.

When her apartment rent came due, she moved out. Instead of spending her savings, she sold her furniture and added the money to her saving's account. She bunked in a homeless shelter a few times but was unable to sleep with strangers wandering around all night.

For three months she had been living in her car, which was safer and more comfortable than a cardboard box. But sleeping in a locked car was hot in the summer and would be too cold in Knoxville's winter.

She pulled the red baseball cap over her black, bushy hair, locked the car and went to the hospital cafe for breakfast. A man opened the back door, and said, "Get out of here."

She backed off and waited. When the cooks started serving lunch at 11:00 a.m., her contact put a sack of leftovers on the back steps. It was good to have friends in high places. She grabbed the sack and walked to the bridge to eat.

"Goodness, Honey. Where did you come from?" she said to a young woman wearing a hospital gown, crouched down under the bridge. "You lost, or something?"

The woman shrunk back and didn't say anything.

"You can't go around with your butt hanging out. Come with me. I may have something in the car that'll fit you. I doubt it, though. I'm a size twenty. You look like a size four."

She reached to put her hand on the woman's back. The woman pulled back.

"I won't hurt you. Do I look like I'd hurt you? I know I might not look like your number one citizen, but I ain't gonna hurt nobody. Come on. You need some clothes."

The overalls hung on the woman like they were on a broomstick. Delta helped tuck in the hospital gown, tied a sash from an old robe around her waist, and rolled up the pant's legs.

"There. That'll do for now. What's your name, honey. Can't you talk?" When the woman didn't answer, Delta continued. "Don't make no difference to me if you don't talk. And, it's okay with me if you stole a hospital gown. But, you should 'a got some britches and shoes."

Delta rummaged through her car trunk. "Try on these loafers. Were you in the hospital for treatment?"

The woman put on the shoes and didn't say anything.

"I don't blame you for leaving the hospital. Doctors and nurses are always poking you with needles filled with God knows what. Here." Delta gave her a ham and biscuit sandwich.

The woman gagged after one bite.

"Hey. Give that back. For Pete's sake. If you're gonna live out here, you gotta' learn not to waste food. Long as you don't give me no trouble, you can bunk in my back seat. Poor thing. No telling what they did to you. What's wrong with you? Are you pregnant? Any old boys been messing with you?"

The woman frowned and stared into space.

"I'm Delta. What's your name, Honey?"

"I don't know," the woman whispered, her eyes blank.

"Yeah? Well, now. That's better. You can talk if you have to. I'll call you Priss," Delta said.

"Better than Unknown."

She followed Delta around, watched her trade a few things, including her hospital gown for a pink, long-sleeved sweater. Around supper time Delta picked up a sack of burgers and fries from the back door of McDonald's. They sat on the hood of the car until late evening when Delta unlocked the car doors and got in.

"Get in. I'm locking up for the night. If anybody tries to get in, wake me. You hear?"

Priss pushed a lot of junk out of the way and lay in the back seat listening to Delta talking about going south for the winter. Priss could go if she wanted to.

"Sure hope you ain't pregnant. That would complicate matters considerably. Course we wouldn't just toss it out. A woman who throws her baby away ain't worth the salt in her food. It might even be good to have a kid around. I've got a sister with a gang of young'uns. Ain't no room for me there. Anyhow, I think she's ashamed of me now that I'm on the streets. Folks are like that. When you're down and out, they won't have anything to do with you, even if you're kin."

Finally, Delta was snoring in the front seat. Priss stared through the car window at the clear, night sky where stars twinkled, like her mind had done when Delta mentioned a child. She seemed to remember seeing the tops of trees, dark woods, fog, and then stars. When she finally closed her eyes, sparks flickered behind her eyelids like fireworks on New Year's Eve.

Simon had been on wild goose chases before, but this was a little different. The UT Hospital in Knoxville had no record of admitting an unknown woman Saturday morning like the police report said. Nor had they admitted anyone named Abby Crowley. He checked all the clinics and hospitals in Knoxville and came up empty handed. There was a lot of confusion surrounding this case, but it was more like mis-communication and screw-ups than foul play. The woman found on Highway 68, was Abby. He would bet on it. But how did she get there? Where was she now?

He was hoping no one had told Zack about the woman found on Highway 68. He wanted to be the one to tell him. First he would stop by High Plains Police Department, tell O'Dell his police report was wrong, and see if anybody knew where the woman was taken. He'd probably have to contact the medics. Heading south on U.S. Highway 129 near Maryville, he saw a Blount Memorial Hospital sign. He pulled in the parking lot, took out Abby's driver's license photo and headed to admissions.

Zack was sitting in the yard when the sun peeked over the mountains, waiting for Sammy to wake up.

After breakfast, he and Sammy walked down the gravel road to Oliver's house. About half way there, he lifted Sammy to his shoulders and started singing "Old McDonald had a farm..."

"You're spoiling that boy," Minnie yelled from the porch.

"Let him be, Minnie," Oliver whispered.

"I don't mean any harm," she said. "It's a pleasure to see a child loved so much. That's all spoiling is. Loving."

"And, you want to do the spoiling and the loving," he said, and yelled, "Good morning. How about some coffee and cocoa?"

"That sounds great," Zack said. He took Sammy from his shoulders and sat him down in a rocker on the porch. "The dew was heavy last night. Almost like rain."

"Yeah. The leaves are shedding fast this year. Trees are almost bare," Oliver said.

Minnie brought out a tray and said, "I don't see how you run a business with Sammy in your lap all the time. Why don't you let me keep him?"

Sammy moved closer to Zack to drink his cocoa.

"We're doing fine. He sleeps good at night and takes a nap during the day. That gives me plenty of time to work."

"I'd be tickled to keep him. Come on Sammy. Let's go see the rabbits," Minnie said, sensing the men needed to talk.

Sammy clung to Zack and wouldn't budge.

"Go with Minnie and see the rabbits," Zack said. "I'll be here when you get back. I promise."

Sammy took Minnie's hand, turning his head as he walked away to see if Zack was still there.

"Everybody in this area is looking for Abby," Oliver said. "Any word from Simon, or the police?"

"No. I expect Simon to call today, which is why I don't want to be away from the phone too long."

"It's a pity cell phones don't work in these mountains."

"Maybe that'll be my next project, putting up repeater stations," Zack said.

"It'd take a lot of stations. You'd probably need one on every mountain and there are plenty of those around."

"Cell phones would be worth their weight in gold up here."

"Sure would cost a lot of money," Oliver said.

"Make a lot, too," Zack said.

"Leave it to you to fall into another money making scheme," Oliver said and smiled. "I can't help but feel responsible for Abby's disappearance."

"It's my fault. I brought her here. If I need to go out of town, could you and Minnie stay at my house so Sammy will be in familiar surroundings?"

"I see no problem with that. But, like most kids, he'll probably be okay once you're out of sight," Oliver said.

"Minnie could invite Nita June and her two boys over. But, I'm getting ahead of myself. Simon will find Abby," Zack said.

"Yeah. She'll turn up soon," Oliver said.

"Far as business goes, I'd rather work at home. Anywhere I go around here, Sammy can go with me."

"Well, if anything comes up, we're here. We'll help any way we can," Oliver said, as Minnie approached with Sammy.

"I appreciate it," Zack said, took Sammy and headed home.

As usual, time got away from them roaming in the woods. As soon as Sammy had a bath, he fell asleep watching TV on the couch. A few minutes after Zack put him to bed, Simon's car pulled up in the driveway.

"I was beginning to think you were lost, too," Zack said.

"I've got some good news and some bad news," Simon said.

Zack's eyes narrowed and his lips pressed together.

"I believe she's alive," Simon said.

"I know she's alive. What else have you found?"

"Something very interesting. An unknown woman was found close to the Polk County line early Saturday morning. The police report said she was airlifted to UT. But, they have no record. Neither did any other clinics or hospitals in Knox County. As I was coming home, I saw a Blount Memorial Hospital sign. Not even in Knox County, now mind you. I stopped and learned that an unknown woman was admitted there early Saturday morning, delivered by ambulance. I believe the police report is wrong and the unknown at Blount was Abby."

"What do you mean, was Abby? Didn't you see her?" Zack said, getting up from his lounger, ready to go.

"No. There's a small problem. The bad news."

"What kind of problem?"

"They lost her."

"How can a hospital lose somebody?" Zack sat back down.

"According to a nurse, their unknown was in shock and didn't know who she was. She kept trying to leave, so the doctor kept her heavily sedated. After seeing Abby's driver's license photo, the nurse seemed pretty sure it was the unknown. The unknown was there at 4:00 a.m., but gone when the graveyard shift left at seven."

"How could she leave if she was sedated? You think she was kidnapped? I'll bet she's somewhere around the hospital."

"Somebody could have taken her. But, my guess is she didn't take her medication and left on her own. That happens. What's strange, nobody around the hospital has seen her."

"Jesus. This is unbelievable. What's next?"

"Is there a chance her husband from Chicago could have found her? Does he know where she is? Has he ever seen you?"

"No way," Zack said. "Wait a minute. He saw me briefly in the park. He couldn't possibly make the connection. That was before Abby and I got acquainted."

"You got any food in the house? I'm starved."

"You don't looked starved," Zack said and poked Simon gently in his belly.

"Tell me how you met Abby and how she and Sammy wound up here. Don't leave out anything."

After two sandwiches, a pot of coffee, and hearing the entire story, including the park, Simon said, "Scratch that theory. I've thought from the beginning, somebody picked her up. Now I think they dropped her off south of here at the Polk County line where the truckers found her."

"Have you looked there?" Zack said.

"Yep. The police have covered the scene thoroughly. The evidence was pretty much destroyed by the weather and people walking all over the crime scene before they got it roped off. I think Maryville is the place to look. It seems an older nurse named Norma took a special interest in the unknown. She was working the graveyard shift when the unknown was admitted, and she reported her missing. Reckon you and Sammy can visit Norma? She'll be on duty at seven Wednesday morning."

"I thought you said she was on the graveyard shift."

"She usually works days. She was covering for a friend on that particular weekend."

"We'll all go together in the morning," Zack said.

"I'm leaving in a few minutes. You'll need to go in your car. You got some old, ragged, dirty clothes I can wear?"

"Do I look like I keep old, ragged, dirty clothes?"

"Just give me an old casual outfit you don't want. I'll take care of the ragged and dirty part. And, throw in a jacket. It's cold at night."

"What are you up to, Simon?" Zack said and led the way upstairs to his closet.

"I'm going to sleep on the streets for a few nights."

"Christ. I think I can pay for a motel room."

"You're missing my point."

Zack turned and stared at Simon.

"Oh, my God. No."

Chapter Thirteen

Thad analyzed the documents spread out on his desk. Under the circumstances, investigators had done a good job. The crime scene had been a mess. Everything in and around the Cherokee National Forest was soaked from the heavy fog. Leaves were falling by the truckloads, and a thirty-mile-an-hour wind was blowing the leaves to kingdom come. As if that weren't enough tourists, and neighbors were popping up all over the scene.

Still, the crew had managed to find a cigarette butt and five shoe prints, four of which were probably the perpetrators. The other was a small brogan print trailing off in the woods, along with big paw prints. Probably a kid and a dog that got behind the crime tape. No telling if the brogan prints belonged to the victim. They didn't get around to taking her print before shipping her off to the wild blue yonder. Nobody seemed to remember if she was wearing shoes.

Thad rubbed his freshly shaven chin, picked up the phone and called the examiner.

"So, you think there were four perpetrators."

"That's what it looks like." The examiner explained that the four prints came from shoes or boots with heavy-tread, blue-collar-worker type, not police or medical issue. According to the police, the civilians wore sneakers or loafers, like they would wear around the house, or on vacation, not what they would wear on a hike through the mountains and none of them got behind the crime tape. Other determining factors were tire tracks from a single vehicle that had been parked farther in the woods than the official vehicles. The type of vehicle, or type of tires on the vehicle, could possibly be determined from those tracks.

"Can you tell if the shoe prints trailing off into the woods were there prior to the truckers?"

"Not with the elemental conditions. It's a wonder we found them at all."

"The report mentioned an ambulance. I understood the woman was air lifted to UT."

"The ambulance and helicopter were there. Don't know which one took her. Nor where."

"Any chance to get a report on the tires today?"

"Already got a rush on it, Sheriff."

Thad hung up the phone. *Extra prints on the crime scene? Where did they take her? How did they take her? Ambulance, or helicopter? God forbid the media get wind of this.*

He called O'Dell.

"There seems to be a bit of confusion here. Did you say the helicopter took the woman to UT?"

"No, Sheriff. I said she was already in the ambulance when the helicopter arrived. She didn't appear to be in serious or immediate danger, so she probably went in the ambulance."

"Did the ambulance take her to UT?"

"I didn't ask where they were taking her. By then some thirty-odd civilians had come out of the woodwork and I was busy securing the crime scene."

"Who was with you?"

"I was by myself at the time."

"Does anybody know where the woman is and how she's doing?"

O'Dell said, "I'll see if I can find out."

"Let me know."

Thad scratched his neck, ran his fingers through his thick, red hair, leaned back and tapped a pencil on his desk. One runaway woman. One molested. One missing in a helicopter or ambulance. Could they all be the same woman? How could anybody manage to lose the same woman three times? This was a bigger mess than the firebug in the national forest last fall. There was confusion in the department, to say the least. Maybe they had been a little too excited, being used to petty theft, small possession, parking, speeding tickets, and at most, domestic disturbance.

By six o'clock Zack was halfway to Blount Memorial Hospital. Sammy was strapped in his car seat, pointing at a field, probably the first live cows he'd ever seen. He clapped his hands when a dump truck full of gravel passed by.

Zack doubted that he would get much information about the unknown woman, even if she were Abby. The privacy act prevented authorities from revealing personal information, except in rare cases, maybe to family. She had no kin. Well, Sammy. And Bob, which, of course was out of the question under any circumstance. He hoped Sammy's presence would put Norma in a compassionate, talkative, and hopefully a motherly mood.

Admittance directed him to the nurse's station on the first floor where he took a seat and waited. Shortly after the day crew arrived, a tall, forty-ish nurse approached.

"I'm Norma. You wanted to see me?"

"I was hoping you could tell me something about the unknown woman you admitted last Saturday morning."

"Yes, of course. They said a private investigator had been asking questions about a missing woman who might be our unknown. You must be the husband," she said.

"I'm Zack," he said, not sure what Simon had told them about the husband.

Norma looked at Sammy. "And who's this nice young man?"

"This is Sammy."

"I didn't realize there was a child," Norma whispered, then turned and said, "Hey, Sammy. Let's go see what we can find in our play room."

Sammy clung to Zack.

That's right, Son. Hang on. Paint a perfect picture so it won't be necessary to discuss daddies, husbands and friends.

"He hasn't let me out of his sight since his mother has been gone," Zack said.

"I can imagine," Norma said.

Zack took Sammy's hand and followed to a room that had several small tables with matching chairs. Shelves around the walls bulged with stuffed animals and toys. Sammy grabbed a dump truck and sat down in the floor, filled it with blocks and dumped them back into the box.

"He likes trucks. Where did you find that one?"

"I'm not sure. Most of our toys are donated. You might look at Foothills Mall. There's a nice toy shop there."

Zack took out a copy of Abby's driver's license picture.

"Is this your unknown woman?"

"Driver's license photos are never very good. But that certainly looks like her to me," Norma said.

"Did she say what happened to her? Was she okay?"

"She didn't seem to know what happened. I don't believe she spoke at all. She seemed confused and afraid of something, or somebody. Getting out of bed and leaving was the only thing on her mind. That's why we kept her sedated. Apparently not enough, though, since she's gone. I'm surprised she had the strength to leave. She wouldn't eat. I kept hoping she'd remember her name. But she didn't. Not that I know of."

That was odd. Abby had the appetite of a horse. He never understood how a person so tiny could eat so much.

"I'll go get her clothes. They had to cut off her jeans. The zipper was stuck," Norma said.

While Norma was gone, Zack wrote his home phone numbers on the back of his business card. When she returned, he said, "My private numbers are on the back. Will you call if you think of anything that might help us find her?"

"I certainly will, Zack. Good luck," Norma said.

Zack took the clothes, picked up Sammy, and left. *That went well. Simon was right. The Unknown was Abby. If she was too weak to leave, did someone remove her physically? Surely not. Why would anyone do that? Why would she leave on her own?*

After driving around, scanning the area, Zack stopped at the Foothills Mall and bought the biggest dump truck they had. From there he went to the Waffle House, where he ordered ham, grits, eggs, toast and blackberry jelly, Sammy's favorite. While the boy ate, he called Simon's cell number.

No answer. Probably turned it off, or left it in the car. Homeless people don't usually carry cell phones.

Feeling good in one way, let down in another, he strapped Sammy in his car seat and headed back to the mountains.

Why does she keep running away, leaving hospitals, going off into the wild blue yonder? Apparently she can't face reality. Life either, for that matter. What about good old Zack? Can he face reality, handle life? No problem. He can handle anything. Well, he'd better find a solution, or he'll be raising the son he's always wanted. Alone.

"You're out early this morning," Minnie said as Zelphie came up the porch steps. "How long you been walking?"

"You know I don't own a watch. Lie down, Peach." The Rottweiler lay on her stomach with her paws out front.

"Can I get you something?"

"Don't need a thing," Zelphie said.

"You look tired," Minnie said.

"I'm thinking about Abby. Zack must be out of his mind. Heard anything new?"

"The private detective has a lead. We won't know anything until Zack gets back. He and Sammy went to the Blount Memorial to see if their unknown woman is Abby."

"I can't believe she just walked off."

"You of all people should understand that. Maybe she was nervous like you, Zelphie, and needed to walk."

"But she left her son. Is he okay?"

"They say she thought he was dead and sort of went crazy with grief. He's doing fine. Keeps asking if anybody's seen his ma. Won't let Zack out of his sight. Nobody would know Sammy's not his own. Never seen a man take on so."

"Reckon why anyone would want to hurt Abby?"

"Hurt her? What makes you think someone hurt her, Zelphie? Are you having a bad spell, or do you know something?"

"I'm just tired, I guess."

"Zelphie. If you saw anything suspicious, or unusual during your walks, it's your obligation to tell the police."

"If I went around telling what I see that's suspicious and unusual they'd lock me in a looney bin. People do weird stuff, Minnie. All the time. Best to keep what I see to myself."

"Lord have mercy. You know something," Minnie said.

"I know a lot of people will be hurt before this is over. I never met Abby, but they say she's real nice."

"She's as nice as they come. Beautiful, inside and out."

"You got a picture of her?"

"Why, no. But she's a precious little thing. Not much bigger than her son. Blond hair like his, too."

"If I had a pack of cigarettes, I'd smoke 'em all at one setting," Zelphie said. "You say a private eye has a lead?"

"That's what Zack told Oliver," Minnie said.

"Did Zack hire him?"

"I don't imagine he had to hire him. He's Zack's friend, Simon Freely."

"I know him. Simon and Zack are friends with my lawyer, Charlie Donelson."

"I didn't know you had a lawyer."

"Yes you do. He handled my boundary line mess."

"Seems I do remember that."

"Well, Abby ain't in these mountains. I've walked all over them since she went missing."

"You better go home and rest, Zelphie. First thing we know, you'll have a heart attack somewhere in the wilderness and we'll all be looking for you," Minnie said.

"My heart's as strong as an ox. I'll rest when I'm dead."

"You're no spring chicken."

"I know how old I am, Minnie. My age has nothing to do with this conversation."

"I'm just saying you should take care of yourself."

"That's what I'm doing when I'm walking. Come on, Peach."

The old woman headed down the mountain with the dog by her side, a stick in her hand, and a heavy burden on her back.

Priss opened her eyes. Her bed was bouncing. No. The world was moving. She threw up her hands. Too late. She slid off the back seat and landed in the floorboard among boxes of clothes, shoes, pots, pans, groceries and such. The car swerved around a sharp curve, then another. Finally the hum of the engine quieted as the car slowed and the ride became smooth. She lay still. There were no streetlights, only the dim dash lights revealing the car's gray ceiling. She got up from the floorboard and rested her arms on the back of the front seat. Through the windshield she watched the black top zooming beneath the car. Curve after curve. Then, thick fog. Trees. Lots of trees that came right up to the road. Pain shot through her head. Lights flashed on and off in her mind. Faces, coming and going. Hands fumbling all over her body. White sheets and needles. She grabbed her head and screamed, "No."

"Good. You're awake. Get up here and keep me company," Delta said, hanging on to the steering wheel with both hands.

"We're in the woods. No." Priss moaned like she was dying.

"What's wrong with you?" Delta pulled the car over on the narrow shoulder of the road.

This gal is slightly one can short of a six-pack. Good ole, Delta. No. Stupid, dumb, Delta. Why don't you just go out and take in some more idiots? Fill your car with crazies.

"Don't stop. Go. Go," Priss screamed.

"It's okay, Priss. The doors are locked. Ain't nothin' out here but a few wild animals. They're more afraid of you than you are of them."

Priss froze. "That's what he said." She looked out into the wilderness.

"He who?"

Priss screamed, "Drive. Keep driving." Her head was splitting.

Her stomach was doing flips. "Go." Such pain.

"Okay. Okay. Calm down. I'm driving. See?" Delta pulled back onto the road.

Priss climbed into the front seat. "Why did we move?"

"God-o-mighty. You were screaming, telling me to drive."

"No. I mean before. We were at the bridge."

"I'm going south for the winter. Don't you remember nothing I tell you?"

"I don't know if I should go."

"News flash. Too late. You were asleep. I couldn't just drag you out, dump you on the ground and drive off, could I?"

"But, it's night. You were supposed to be sleeping."

"Yeah. Well, I had insomnia."

"Look. It's a U.S. Highway sign. Number 129."

"So?" Delta said.

"That was on my test."

Tests? Highway signs? Brilliant. This nut is just plain brilliant. Yep. Delta. You've picked a real winner. Probably not from a hospital at all. More like an escapee from a mental ward somewhere. Or, an alien from outer space. Sitting right here beside me. Taking over my life. Screaming. Asking questions. Telling me not to stop. To drive.

"Won't me to drive? I have a license," Priss said.

Now, it-wants-to-drive. No thank you. Duh!

"Yeah? Well, where is this license?"

"I don't know."

"Is it on your person? You cannot drive a car without a license on your person. Understand?"

"Oh. I forgot," Priss said. "Where are we going?"

"South, Priss. Just south. South on U.S. Highway 129."

"I don't think I've ever been south."

"Yeah? Well, that's a breakthrough, Priss. Happen to know where you have been? Got a news flash on that concept?"

Priss didn't say anything for a long time.

Delta looked at her passenger. Her mouth fell open and she slowed the car. Priss's face was like stone. Absolutely no emotion. Yet, her cheeks were soaking wet, like someone had doused her with a bucket of water. Tears. Big tears of pain dripping down, wetting the pink sweater Delta had traded for the hospital gown. More tears than Delta had ever seen on one person's face.

Delta's heart was in her throat. Obviously, Priss had more inner pain and trouble than she knew how to handle. She was sorry she called her a nut. She wouldn't do it again. That was a promise she made to herself, and to God. She reached out and lightly touched Priss's hand.

"Don't worry, Priss. It's okay. We'll find warm weather. Everything will be just fine."

What in the world have they done to you, Priss? Hang on. I'll reach you, honey. I'll pull you out of that hellhole. I'll get in your head and we'll figure it all out together.

Chapter Fourteen

After a home burglar alarm went off, O'Dell and Anderson sped to a country estate and were greeted by five dogs. One was the size of a pony. The deputies cautiously got out of the car and made their way around the house. The side door was open. No forced entry. Inside were four more dogs making themselves at home. The door apparently had not been closed good, and the pets had pushed it open.

In a few minutes, the owner's mother arrived. She couldn't tell if anything was missing. The TV and stereo were intact and that's usually what thieves took first. The mother said that strangers, and most friends, wouldn't get out of the car with so many dogs in the yard, and the dogs always had the run of the place. This confirmed the deputies' theory about the dogs pushing open the door.

Back at the office, Anderson inherited phone duty while O'Dell went to lunch. Eager to show her expertise after being on the job only a month, she carefully wrote a report on the alarm call and was reviewing her work when the phone rang.

"The four involved in the crime live in this area," a muffled voice said and the phone went dead.

I probably shouldn't call the Chief. I'll call O'Dell at High Plains Cafe, interrupt his lunch.

"Probably just a kook," O'Dell said. "What'd they say?"

Anderson repeated the phone message.

"Hmm. That could be something." With his shoulder holding the phone, he pulled out money and payed for lunch. "Was the caller male or female?"

"Couldn't tell. The voice was muffled."

"The four involved...Where did the call come from?"

"One of the pay phones at The Prize."

"I'm heading there right now."

"Should I come?" Julie said.

"You man the office. No pun intended," he said.

He pulled into the parking lot at The Prize, which was a combination service station, convenient store and a roasted chicken deli with booths. A man using one of the two pay phones said he'd been talking about five minutes and no one had used the other phone. O'Dell wrote down the number the man had called for verification, then headed back to the office. *Why of all days did he eat at High Plains Cafe instead of The Prize?*

Simon turned on his cell phone and opened his notebook computer. With the hobo clothes in a plastic bag, he took a fifteen-minute shower, scrubbing until his skin was red. He slipped on his robe, scanned his notes and called Zack.

"Could be good news, depending on how you look at it. The homeless on the streets haven't seen Abby and she hasn't stayed at any of the shelters. A Blount Memorial cafe worker said a woman has been picking up leftovers for several months."

"That can't be Abby. She hasn't been missing that long."

"No. But maybe Abby's with her."

"What makes you think that?"

"Instinct. The woman stopped picking up food two days ago. No one knew her name, where she was from, nor why she stopped getting food. I've got some thoughts, but not worth talking about. I just wanted to let you know I'm at the Airport Motel tonight. Don't know where I'll go from here."

"I need to find someone to keep Sammy."

"Why? You can't do anything yet. I'll be in touch."

Zack sat with his elbows on the breakfast bar. He should be in Denver for the opening of his new office. Sammy would enjoy the airplane ride. Taking Sammy to meetings would be fun, but might raise a few eyebrows. Of course, he could always get someone to sit with Sammy in the room. Or, he could just leave him with Minnie.

"Why can't Mommy keep me?" Sammy said. He had the habit of appearing out of nowhere.

"Mommy's not here. Don't you like staying with me?"

"You don't want to keep me anymore."

"Of course I do. Where did you get that idea?"

"You said you need to find somebody to keep Sammy."

I'll have to be more careful. Little heads have big ears.

"Yes I did. But not because I don't want to keep you. I thought you might want to play with someone your age."

"Like Frank and Billy?"

"Yeah," Zack said.

"We could invite them over," Sammy said.

"Now why didn't I think of that? Why don't you watch TV while I finish up my work, then we'll see what we can do."

With Sammy settled in front of the TV, Zack called Thad. He hung up thinking the sheriff was not doing his job, or not telling Zack everything. Law men. Won't say anything until they have the facts. At least, they seemed to be trying to find the abductors, if, in fact, she was abducted. He called Minnie.

"Are there any childcare centers in Soda Creek?"

"I hadn't thought much about it, Zack. Why are you looking for a childcare center?"

"I think Sammy needs to be with kids his age. Reckon Nita June would keep him for a few days?"

"Absolutely not. A dog wouldn't be safe in that house."

"Why do you say that?"

"Because it's a fact."

"Hmm." He thought about what Abby said about Nita June having a problem that she didn't want to talk about. "Well, I was thinking more of hiring her to stay here so Sammy could play with her sons."

"Frankly, I'm hurt. No. I'm mad. You know I want to keep Sammy. Obviously, you don't think I'm good enough."

"That is absolutely not true, Minnie. He's a handful. Are you sure a child his age won't be too much for you?"

"Don't be ridiculous. He's no trouble at all," Minnie said, with a sudden coolness in her voice.

"How soon can you be here?"

"As soon as you need me."

"Okay. When I get my itinerary, I'll be in touch."

If Sammy were his, he'd take him to the meetings, sit him in the head chair and tell everybody how smart he is. But, Sammy wasn't his. With Abby missing, somebody might could accuse him of kidnapping. He'd ask his lawyer.

After working a couple of hours in the office, he packed his bag and put it by the door. He went to Sammy's room and laid down on the twin bed. He'd be home in a couple of days. Maybe then, together, he and Sammy would look for Abby. *It's a plan. The best one he had at the moment.*

Billy and Frank were in bed and Nita June was washing the supper dishes. Her husband was watching football with one ear to the phone, probably sharing plays of the game with one of his buddies. She didn't know what had come over him, but she enjoyed the attention, like when they got married, before the boys and the bills and the drinking.

"What's wrong, now?" her husband said into the phone. "Hold your horses. I'll be there in ten minutes."

He grabbed his camouflage jacket, pecked Nita June's cheek.

"How long will you be gone," she said.

"Now you know better'n to ask me that, Darlin'. You jus' keep the bed warm," he said, whacked her rear and left.

Arty pulled his car off Highway 68 and drove a good hundred feet into the forest on an old logging road. He parked, turned off the lights and waited.

"It's been fifteen minutes. Reckon he's coming?" Arty said.

"Probably had trouble getting out of the house," Nick said.

"I hope he knows what to do about Larry's sudden attack with religion," Arty said.

"Larry's attack ain't sudden. He's always had more religion than he needs."

"But he's gittin' down right spooky these days," Arty said.

"Larry was born weird. Hush. Somebody's coming."

A car turned off the highway, pulled in the logging road and stopped. The headlights went off and the driver got out.

"What's so all fired important that you're draggin' me out in the middle of the night? I'm missing the game."

"I think Larry's losing it. He might talk," Arty said.

"Maybe we ought'a send him out of town for a couple of months," Nick said.

"Or, permanent like."

"We ain't having nothing to do with permanent," Nick said.

Fifteen minutes of yelling and they agreed to meet and try to talk some sense into Larry.

"After our meeting, we'll swear we haven't seen each other in a month, except at work. I've been home every night since my wife threatened to leave me a month ago."

"She threatened to leave you?" Arty said.

"No. Stupid. That's what he's gonna say. That's gonna be his story," Nick said.

"Oh. And what's gonna be our story, Nick?"

"That's what we've got to figure out."

"Whatever you come up with, you ain't seen me. I've been home with my wife every night. Git it?"

The sun glared off the hood of the car as Delta passed through a pit stop town where one small gas station was closed up tighter than Dick's hatband. She had thought about driving down I-75 through Chattanooga, but decided cutting through the mountains would be more fun, less traffic, less cops. Not that she was afraid of cops. She liked cops. She just wanted to avoid hassles and tickets and such. Contending with her passenger had kept her from reaching the intended destination by daylight. Didn't matter. She wasn't punching a time clock.

"I'm gonna have a wreck if I don't get some sleep," she said to Priss, who was sitting like a stump, eyes glued to the road. "It's daylight. You gonna flip out if I stop?"

No answer.

"Okay, then. I'll take that as a good sign." She pulled into an area where a couple of picnic tables sat beside a creek.

Tourists pay for this scenery. Does Priss see the beauty, or will she freak out when it gets dark? I'll probably have to leave at sundown. And I'm not crazy about driving at night.

"Let's stretch our legs, Priss. I need to go to the bushes, if you know what I mean. My bladder's about to burst."

She came back, fumbled in the floorboard and pulled out a bag of potato chips, some cheese crackers and two sodas.

"Breakfast on the road by a stream," she said, spread her feast on one of the wood tables and took a seat. "I realize it's not the hospital cafe, but campers ain't supposed to eat regular food while they're camping. Wonder how long we can stay here. Probably run out of food before anybody notices us."

Priss didn't speak, just stared into space.

After breakfast, Delta led Priss to the passenger seat, got under the wheel and locked the doors.

"Wake me in an hour," Delta said and pulled her cap down over her eyes. "Then we'll talk about staying here a few days before we go on to explore the unknown."

"I'm unknown," Priss said.

Delta pushed pack her cap and looked at the statue sitting next to her in the passenger seat.

God. You've probably forgotten me by now. I ain't exactly kept in touch. Yeah. Yeah. I know you've heard me complaining. Forget that. This ain't about me. It's about this lost child. You must have dumped her in my lap for a reason. So, tell me. What am I supposed to do with her?

Zelphie woke up at four in the morning, unable to move. Two days earlier, she headed to town and had walked five miles when

Mrs. Giles picked her up and drove her to the grocery store. Mrs. Giles offered to bring her home after she finished shopping. Zelphie lied, said she was meeting Minnie.

Lord. I'm sorry I lied. I'm sorry about lots of things.

After buying a few groceries and making a phone call, she started home. She was about to cut through the woods to shorten her trip when Minnie drove up beside her and stopped.

"What are you doing ten miles from home?"

"I needed a few things."

"I've told you a hundred times, I'll bring you shopping."

"Mrs. Giles brought me in," Zelphie said.

"Well, a fine thing she did, leaving you to walk home. Get in. And that dog. Does he have to go everywhere you go? Tell him to get in the back of the truck. Ain't room in the cab for that big hunk of meat. I bet he'd rip a person to pieces for looking at you crossways. Traipsing the woods like you do he's just what you need. He's as good a friend as any, I reckon."

"He's a she," Zelphie said.

That was two days ago. Two days she could hardly move. She had always figured she'd die alone. Suddenly, she didn't want it that way. She had to talk to the sheriff, or somebody.

You're not going to die, Zelphie. Rest. You'll be better when you wake up.

Chapter Fifteen

"You make it sound like we're plotting to over-throw the government, Zack," Minnie said. "As usual, you're inviting the guilt of the world to rest on your shoulders. Looking forward to your return will be much easier for Sammy to accept than the fear of you leaving. Trust me. He'll be fine."

Oliver's bushy eyebrows raised as he smiled and looked at Zack. After thirty years with the woman, he knew how convincing she could be. In this case, he agreed with her.

"Okay, Minnie," Zack said. "But the guilt will fall on your shoulders if your plan doesn't work."

Sammy was used to going for rides with Oliver and Minnie. After the truck was out of sight, Zack left for Denver. He called Sammy from the Knoxville airport before boarding the plane and daily while he was gone. Minnie had been right. Sammy was no trouble and was excited about Zack's return.

On the way home from Denver Zack visited Thad, who had new leads, but wouldn't discuss the investigation. From there, Zack drove south to the area where the truckers had found the unknown woman. He walked around thinking about Abby and the past four months. He had taken her from a hopeless situation and dropped her in another as bad, or worse. He had to find her, let her know Sammy was okay. *But, if she doesn't know who she is, will she remember Sammy? Or me?*

From there he drove to the little church, and remembered the minister had resigned a month ago. He had been a young fire and brimstone preacher, eager to fill the church with newly converted sinners. The deacons, who had been members all their lives, their parents before them, weren't concerned with increasing affiliation. So the young preacher took the podium one Sunday morning, said he didn't feel like he was fulfilling his mission. It was time to move on. He obviously hadn't discussed departure with his wife. She seemed shocked, like the deacons, who urged him to stay, but weren't worried when he refused. Visiting preachers were handling services until God sent the right man.

As always Zack became calm, sitting on the back pew. He felt so comfortable there, you'd think his name was on the bench. *Father. Lead us to Abby. Protect her. Give her and little Sammy some happiness. They've been through so much. I'm ever thankful for Your blessings. Amen.*

Zelphie's twenty by thirty, one-room cabin sat in the thicket down a wagon trail a quarter of a mile off the gravel road. The rough-cut hemlock exterior was gray with age and almost invisible among the trees. The front of the cabin faced east, its lean-to, shingle roof sloped to the west. A few years back Zelphie had the out-house torn down and plumbing installed.

She had a bathroom enclosed in the corner opposite the small stone fireplace, which was next to her bed, loveseat, dining table with two chairs and cooking stove.

"It's too dark in here," Minnie said, pushing back the yellow curtains covering the shiny windows. Everything sparkled like it had been scrubbed with Lysol. "Lord have mercy, you're killing yourself. If you're no better by morning, I'm taking you to the doctor. And I'll have no back talk."

"Lives will be destroyed because I know," Zelphie said.

"Whose lives? What are you talking about now?"

"I saw, but I didn't see," Zelphie said.

"What did you see and not see? Something in the woods?"

"I know, I tell you. I know." Her head writhed from side to side. "God's punishing me for what I saw and didn't see. God knows all. I know nothing. Yet, I know too much."

"Take this aspirin." *You've totally flipped this time.*

"Aspirin won't ease my burden. I must remember."

"A nap might help you remember."

"No. Sleeping will make me forget."

"When did you eat last?"

"I don't know."

Minnie pulled her short, straight brown hair behind her ears, found a can of soup in the cabinets and went to work at the two-burner stove. When the soup was hot, she crushed a pill in a bowl, stirred in the liquid and spoon-fed the old lady.

"Of all times for you to get down in the bed. I've got my hands full with Sammy."

"That poor boy," Zelphie said.

"Somebody'll check on you in a little while," Minnie said.

When Zelphie fell asleep, Minnie poured the remaining soup in a bowl and put it in front of Peach lying beside the bed.

"Watch her, dog," she said, pulled a quilt around Zelphie's shoulders, and left.

She drove the truck down the gravel road, stopped outside Nita June's trailer, and honked the horn.

"What brings you to the ridge?" Nita June said, standing in the half open door.

"Zelphie's in a bad way," she yelled from the truck window. "She walked to town a few days ago and it nearly killed her."

"She walks ever' day. Must be somethin' else."

"Whatever it is, she's talking out of her head."

"You think it's the flu?"

"No. There's no fever. She's asleep now. I'd stay with her, but I'm watching Sammy. And of course, I'm staying at Zack's house so the boy won't be scared. Foolish idea, never the less, that's what I'm doing. Go check on her in a little while," Minnie said and drove on.

Oliver heard the truck shift to low coming up the mountain. He met Minnie in Zack's driveway.

"How's she doing?"

"She's talking crazy. I never thought I'd see Zelphie helpless in bed. I figured she'd die somewhere in the woods with that old dog. I can't stand to see her like this. She needs to be looked after. Maybe she ought to be in a home."

"She'd die tomorrow in a home, and you know it."

"I gave her a sleeping pill. She's asleep now."

"Zelphie took a sleeping pill? I'm surprised."

"She didn't know she was taking it. I mixed it with soup."

"Should you give her a sleeping pill?"

"It's just an over-the-counter thing. She needed rest and was fighting sleep. Said sleep would make her forget what she knows but don't know, and what she saw and didn't see."

"What's she talking about?"

"Your guess is as good as mine. Did you take the roast out of the oven? Zack should be home any minute."

"The roast is fine. Zack's in the rose garden with Sammy."

"My word. Fooling with Zelphie has put me behind. I wanted to set the table and pack Sammy's things before he got here."

"Don't get your panties in a bunch. I think Zack and Sammy want to do their own packing."

"I hope they pack warm clothes. It'll be cold this week. Well, don't just stand there, Honey. Help me get things ready."

She opened the door and saw the table was set.

"We were just waiting for you, Sweetie. Sammy set the table. Said you needed help cause you had a lot on your mind."

She bit her lip, pushed up her eyeglasses, wiped her eyes.

"Oh, that sweet boy."

Delta was a city girl living in the woods with nature. And she loved it. She filled empty soda bottles with clear, cold water from the stream. *Free bottled water.*

"This is great, Priss. We don't need money here."

Priss sat staring at a bright orange leaf bumping against rocks as it floated away in the cold water. She hadn't said a word all day. The sun was setting against a clear sky, which meant the moon would be shining. Would it be light enough for Priss? Apparently not. She was getting in the car.

Of course, most people, including herself, was a bit scared in the dark woods. But not crazy scared like Priss. How could she light up the place? She plundered behind the back seat and found a flashlight. The batteries might last until Priss went to sleep. What do campers do? Build fires. Great. A fire for light and heat. She was soon up to her elbows in the trunk, searching for blankets and the matches she had picked up from a fast food place that still allowed smoking.

The car motor cranked.

"What the...?" She looked up. Priss was at the wheel. Before she could move, the car pulled off.

"Come back here, Priss," she screamed. "Mercy."

Standing with her hands on her hips, she watched the car zoom away, the trunk lid flapping up and down. She sat on the picnic table with her feet on the bench. *Well. She said she could drive. And, I'm stranded in the middle of nowhere with no lights, no matches, no blankets, no food. No kidding!*

O'Dell and Anderson were discussing the Harry Potter books and how some were calling them sinful because of the wizards and witches, when the call came in.

"I hope I'm doing right, calling ya'll instead of 911."

"What's the problem?" O'Dell said.

"There's somethin' going on in the barn behind my house."

"Why do you think something's going on?"

"I don't think somethin's goin' on. I know somethin' goin' on. My dogs won't hush. They don't bark like this unless somethin's wrong."

"What's your name, Sir."

"Name's Karr. I live way out on Rafter road." Mr. Karr gave O'Dell directions to his house. "It'll take ya'll a while to git here. I'm goin' on out there with my shotgun."

"You best wait until we get there, Mr. Karr," O'Dell said.

"Naw. If it's a bear, I'll kill it or run it off. If it's a human, well, that's why I'm calling you. I'll hold 'em till you get here," Mr. Karr said and hung up.

"Let's go," O'Dell said. "Ever been to Rafter?"

"No," Anderson said.

"You're in for a treat. You'll love these directions."

Twenty minutes later, Anderson was driving in the middle of a hay field in the woods with the squad car lights flashing.

"We passed the church, took the right fork, turned through the gate into the field. Now what?" Anderson said.

"Cross over the creek on the steel beams and go past three bales of hay."

Anderson looked at him and smiled. "Three bales of hay?"

"Told you you'd love it." O'Dell was grinning. "That's the third bale. Turn right. Hang a left when you come to an old yellow Buick. The barn's just beyond the Buick."

Anderson was giggling. "This is worse than Deliverance."

O'Dell was trying not to laugh out loud. He had turned on the dash light to make sure he had the directions right. He turned off the light and looked up. "There. See? The barn."

"I see it," Anderson said.

They left the car, unsnapped their guns and pushed the barn door open. A man with a shotgun was standing over another man on the floor with a noose around his neck.

"You Mr. Karr?" Anderson said to the man with the shotgun.

"Yeah."

"Is he breathing?" Anderson said.

"Is now. Weren't when I cut 'im down," Mr. Karr said.

"Anderson, radio for an ambulance," O'Dell said, and bent over the unconscious man. "Do you know this man, Mr. Karr?"

"No. Can't say I do," Mr Karr said, standing back while the officer analyzed the scene.

Anderson rushed back in. "Ambulance is on the way," she said and examined the rope and a barrel beside the man.

"Why was a man you don't know hanging himself in your barn?" O'Dell said.

"Can't say I know that either."

"He wasn't hanging himself, O'Dell," Anderson said.

"Then what, pray tell, was he doing with a rope around his neck?"

O'Dell said.

"Look at the height of the barrel and the length of the rope. No way he could have kicked the barrel over. He couldn't reach it. Looks like somebody was helping him."

"What about the ladder?" O'Dell said.

"I put it there to cut 'im down," Mr. Karr said.

"Good thing you came out. Did you see anybody leave?"

"Yeah. Matter of fact, I did. When I turned on the floodlights and started this way with my shotgun, a car spun out across the field. I was too far away to get the plate number, but it was a light brown, Ford sedan, late 80's model."

"Did you see who was in it?" Anderson said.

"I can't give you a description, if that's what you mean. But there were three heads in the car."

Simon checked out of the motel and threw his bags in the car with little thought of where he was going. He would drive around town, think, and follow his instincts. Getting in the head of a male serial killer was easier than determining the mind of a woman. Predicting the movements of a female with amnesia was impossible. Though he didn't know why, he believed Abby hooked up with the woman getting food from the hospital.

Why did the woman stop picking up food? Did she leave in a car? Was she begging food because her apartment rent was due and she had no money? Heck. Maybe she was feeding the neighbor's dog. He drove south on I-75 to Clearwater where Abby first went missing, stopping to show her photo in establishments at every exit. Nobody had seen her. *This doesn't feel right. If the lady has a car, if she left Maryville, she wouldn't come this way. She'd take back roads. Too many 'if's'.* He wheeled across the interstate's grassy median and headed back. *Women. Okay. Forget that part. He couldn't. If he were trailing a man, he'd have found him by now. He needed a female assistant.*

An hour later, he was back at the motel where the young desk clerk smiled and asked if he had missed his flight. Simon stared at him and didn't answer.

"Want the same room, Mr. Freely? It's still available."

"That'll be fine," Simon said, wondering what difference it made which room he had.

After logging the day's activities, he laid back, reviewed the case and wondered if Zack was home from Denver.

O'Dell had filed a report on the hanging the night before. As soon as he woke up, he called the sheriff to make sure he got all the facts this time.

"The medics usually take such cases to UT. When I asked if the man could be treated in Clearwater, they said yes. I told them to take him there, thinking we need him in Monroe county."

"Good thinking, O'Dell. Who was with you?"

"Anderson. She's been here a month. Got a good head for details. Noticed right off that the barrel was too low for the man to stand on to hang himself. We think the hanging is linked with the unknown woman, the missing woman and the phone calls."

"There was more than one call?"

"Two. The callers said almost the same thing."

"Male or female?" the sheriff said.

"That's where it gets a little tricky. Both voices were muffled, but we think it was one male, one female."

"What time do you and Anderson report for duty today?"

"We're on the evening shift," O'Dell said.

"You got plans for the day?"

"I was gonna hang around the house 'til time to go in."

"Did the man have an ID on him?"

"Driver's license. We drove by the address on his license last night. Nobody was home."

"How long will it take you and Anderson to get here?"

"She lives between here and your office," O'Dell said.

"Good. You can go with me to the hospital to see the man."

Chapter Sixteen

"Can Harvey go?" Sammy said.

"Of course. I wouldn't think of leaving Harvey," Zack said.

Sammy had never mentioned his dad. He never played with Willard, who was on the shelf, holding bad memories.

"You won't need all your clothes," Zack said. Sammy had piled the contents of his chest of drawers on the bed and was trying to stuff it all in the small suitcase. "We're coming back. Just bring two of your favorite, warm outfits."

Sammy picked up a Tweety Bird sweat suit, and a pair of flannel-lined jeans and jacket from the pile. "These."

"Good. Put the others back in the drawers and get your pajamas, socks, and toothbrush," Zack said.

After Sammy packed the items, he tried to stuff Harvey in the suitcase.

"Harvey can ride up front with us."

"Can we leave Mommy a note so she can find us?"

Zack choked. "Yes. We'll leave a note."

Sammy struggled to carry his own little bag down the steps. Zack smiled and tossed it in the back of the SUV with his.

"Where does Simon live?" Sammy said, as Zack strapped him into his seat.

"We're meeting him at a motel."

"Like before?" Sammy said.

"Before?"

"You know. When I first saw you."

"It's a different motel."

"Oh. Will it have movies and breakfast? Like before?"

"If that's what you want."

"Yeah," the boy said.

Minnie tried to tell Zelphie a storm was moving in, but she wouldn't listen.

"I must talk to the sheriff," Zelphie said. "Minnie. Get the sheriff. I must tell him."

"There, now. We'll get him in a little while."

"Get him now, Minnie. Please."

"Okay. Then we're going to the doctor."

"No doctor. The sheriff. Please."

The sheriff can't do you no good. I'm getting Oliver and we're taking you to the doctor. If you live, you're coming home with me. You need a caretaker.

The wipers flapped the drizzling rain across the windshield as Minnie drove the truck to Zack's house where Oliver was stacking firewood, preparing for a winter storm expected in twenty-four hours. The forecasters were predicting ice instead of snow for the Soda Creek area, with temperatures below zero. If the storm stalled on the mountains as usual, they would be immobile for days or weeks. Nobody could drive on icy mountain roads. Oliver knew he had to be prepared for anything.

"This will have to wait, Ollie," Minnie said.

"I need to get this done now. The storm…"

"I know about the storm. We have to get Zelphie to the doctor before it hits," Minnie said, and pulled her jacket hood up to keep the cold rain off her eyeglasses.

"She's no better?" Oliver said, looking up from his work.

"She's worse. The crazy old woman wants the sheriff."

"Zelphie may be a lot of things. But, she's not crazy. Wisdom comes with age, Minnie. That makes her the smartest person I know," he said. "Besides you, of course."

"It was just a figure of speech. I didn't mean it."

"If something's bothering her and she needs to talk to Thad, then, we should get him."

"I don't think there's time, Oliver. We need to get her to the doctor. Can we go now?"

Oliver threw down his gloves and pulled out the keys to Zack's house. He knew better than to argue. His wife was very wise and headstrong. Her logic usually outweighed his. But, this time she was too close to the problem to think straight.

"Why are we going in Zack's house?"

"I'm calling the ambulance and Thad," he said and went in the house. "Then, I'm gonna finish stacking the wood."

"We can drive to the hospital quicker than the ambulance can get way out here," Minnie said, following on his heels.

"Okay. I'll tell Thad to meet us at the hospital."

He turned and saw tears on his wife's face.

"There, now," he said and put his arms around her. "I know you love Zelphie like a mother. We'll take care of her. Don't you worry."

Delta ached all over. The picnic table had been a hard bed. It was better than sleeping on the ground. She would probably have pneumonia from shivering all night. Lucky she had on her coat. She splashed her face with icy stream water and did a few stretches to limber up.

Can't blame nobody but myself. It's my fault for picking up strays. Shoulda' left you hunkered under the bridge where I found you. Dumb, dumb. I don't know why I worry about you, Priss. You're pitiful. By golly, you fooled me again. I really thought you'd come back for me. Well, fool on you. The gas tank's empty. What will you do when the gas runs out and you ain't got me to scream at? I'm glad I taped my cash to my belly. Might as well stop fussing and start walking.

As cold as it was, she had worked up a sweat by the time she reached a sign that said four miles to the next town. Only one car had passed since she started walking. She had held out her hand, but the driver didn't even slow down. Nobody stopped for hitchhikers anymore. Hearing a noise, she turned and saw a black Lincoln zoom over the hill. It flew by. Then the brakes screeched. The car backed up. Out stepped a western boot wearing cowboy type, with a hat the size of Texas covering his head. The skyscraper of a man leaned on the car and lifted his sunshades the same color as his permanent suntan.

"Hey," the man said. "You stranded out here or do you just like to walk?"

"It's not my favorite sport." *Mercy. I'm in the twilight zone. Do, do, do, do.*

"I like a gal with a sense of humor. Want a lift?"

"Sounds good to me. Where you goin'?" she said and got in.

"Atlanta," he said, and spun the Lincoln out on the road. "Ever been to a Karaoke contest?"

"Never heard of it." *Dueling banjos and not bad looking.*

"You sing?"

"Only in the shower," Delta said.

"I'm Marshall Dwight Earp. Actually, that's my stage name. Real name's Marshall Dwight Talley. I sing. Country Western."

"You could a' fooled me. I'm Delta Talbot." *God. You let 'em out. I snag 'em in.*

"If you don't have to be anywhere, Delta, you can go with me to Hot-lanta and watch me win the Karaoke contest."

"Actually, I'm looking for my car."

"You lost your car?"

"My friend drove it off last night and didn't come back."

"Not much of a friend to do that," Dwight said.

"Tell me about it."

"I think I'd rather hear your story."

"Yeah? Well, it's too long and I don't want to tell it. Let's just find my car."

"I can do that. Where do you think we should look?"

"Probably along this road somewhere, since the gas tank was empty and my friend didn't have any money. She's, well, a little different, if you get my drift. If we don't see the car, you can drop me at the fist service station."

"So, this friend's a she? That's good news. I think. Do you like guys?"

"Do I look like I like guys?"

"You look like guys like you. You sure you can't sing?"

No, but I bet you could teach me. La, la, la.

"When a man loves a women," he belted out, Charlie Pride style over the humming engine going too fast on mountain roads.

"Whoa. That's it. Stop. That's my car up there."

Pulling over, Dwight said, "Lincoln Continental. Classic. What year is that?"

"It's old," Delta said and hurried to see if the keys were in the ignition. Yep. Everything was intact, except Priss.

Where could that crazy girl be? Sorry, Lord. I promised I wouldn't call her names.

"Come on, Marshall Dwight Earp. Let's get some gas."

"I do like a take-charge woman. Call me Dwight," he said and spun off, singing his music.

"Pull up there. That's her. Sitting on the bench under that street light," Delta said.

"You two ain't gonna' fight, are you?" Dwight said.

"You don't fight with a lost kitten. I'm taking her with me and I'm keeping my keys in my pocket from now on." Delta got out of the car. "Priss. Remember me?"

Priss jumped up, hugged Delta, then sat down on the bench.

"This is Dwight. He's taking us to my car. Come on."

"I can't leave. He said to wait on the bench under the light until he got back," Priss said.

Out of my sight one night and done picked up a pimp.

"Who told you to wait?"

"I don't know," Priss said.

"Maybe you were dreaming. Get in the car," Delta said.

"But he told me to stay until he got back. He was going to get something for me."

"Is he someone you just met, or someone from your past?"

"I didn't just meet anybody."

Know what I think? You're starting to remember. If I push, will I do harm? Maybe I should let it go. No. I should push.

"Think, Priss. Is he a good man or a bad man?"

"He's a good man. He saved me."

That's what all pimps tell pretty young girls.

"You trust me, don't you?" Delta said.

"Yes. You're good to me. Just like him."

"Come on. He'll find you. I'll tell him we had to go," Delta said.

And that ain't all I'm gonna tell him.

"I see what you mean about your friend. She's lucky to have you," Dwight whispered to Delta, driving back to her car.

"Yeah. Well, I don't know which one of us is crazier. Me for picking her up. Or her for…I don't know why the poor thing's crazy. But if I live long enough, I'm gonna find out."

Thad and the deputies stood beside the unconscious man. Rope burns on his neck were not his only body marks. Somebody worked him over good, then tried to hang him.

"O'Dell. Post a guard outside this door, twenty-four-seven," the sheriff said. "It's a shame this had to happen. But if you're right, and I believe you are, this is our first real lead in the case. What's your take on this, Anderson?"

"Same as O'Dell. This man's either involved or knows who is. He was about to talk and they tried to stop him."

"We're going to check his residence, family and place of employment when we leave here," O'Dell said.

"Good. Nurse. Make sure I'm notified of any change in this man's condition. I'm posting a man outside his door. No one is to see him. Absolutely no one, without my say so."

"Do you want his name on the chart?" the nurse said.

"No. Leave him unknown for the time being."

"Okay," the nurse said and left.

"What'd you say was his name?" Thad said to O'Dell.

"Larry Alday."

"That last name sounds familiar. Is he local?"

"Born and raised. Clean record. Never been in trouble. Everybody we've talked to likes him."

"Then, we shouldn't have any trouble. I'll wait and talk to the guard. You go on and check your leads. See if he's got buddies he runs with. See if one of them smokes."

"You're not using special detectives on this?"

"No. I'd like for you both to stay with this case if you don't mind extra hours."

"We don't mind working extra hours at all. It's a real pleasure to work with you, Sir," Anderson said.

"Anderson?"

"Yes, Sir."

"Call me Sheriff. Call me Maloney. Call me Thad, or whatever. But, don't call me Sir."

"Yes Sir. I mean, right. Okay, Sheriff," Anderson said.

O'Dell knew that was coming. Thad was known for being a servant of the people. He turned his head to hide the grin, put on his hat and led the way to the squad car.

Thad stood in the man's room. Sometimes being near a person gave him a better feel for a case. He agreed with the deputies. This man was about to squeal and somebody tried to shut him up. That would explain a lot of things that had been going on in the county lately. There were still some unanswered questions. But it was slowly coming together.

He talked to the guard and was headed to the emergency exit when somebody yelled, "Sheriff."

He turned and saw Oliver running towards him.

"We brought Zelphie Crabtree in. You know. From up in the mountains near our place."

"Yeah. I know Zelphie."

"She was determined to talk to you. Then she got sick. I'm afraid we got here too late for you to find out what she wanted. She's unconscious. This is her doctor," Oliver said.

"What's wrong with her?" Thad said.

"Nothing serious. She's just weak. I expect she'll regain consciousness when she's stronger. She's healthier than people half her age."

"I need you to put her in the room next to the man brought in last night so the guard can watch both doors," Thad said.

"No problem," the doctor said and left.

Oliver was puzzled, but kept quiet. Minnie didn't.

"My Lord, Thad. The woman's eighty-four-years old. She hardly needs a guard. I'll stay and keep an eye on her."

"That's fine and dandy, Minnie. But until she wakes up and I talk to her, I want a guard on the door. Just a precaution," the sheriff said. *What in the world's going on in my county?*

Chapter Seventeen

"I'll hold the bags. You knock," Zack said.

Sammy's knuckles tapped lightly on the door.

"Knock harder. Slap it with your open hand."

Bam. Bam. Bam. He slapped and stood erect like a soldier. When he drew back his hand to slap again, the door swung open.

"You got here early," Simon said.

"Early to bed, early to rise. Our motto," Zack said.

After they had breakfast in the room especially for Sammy, he settled in front of the TV.

"Anything urgent I need to know?"

"Nothing to get excited about."

"Then, you might as well go with us to the zoo," Zack said.

Simon folded his arms across his chest and shook his head. He had seen Zack cope with personal pain while helping others. He had watched him build a business without stepping on the little man. But this was a vulnerable side he didn't recognize. Though it was a strange time to visit animals, he needed to walk with his friend, no matter what.

"Now there's a plan," Simon said. "Take a day off from thinking. See the animals. We'd better bundle up. It's getting cold out there."

While Zack and Sammy ran from cage to cage, Simon showed Abby's photo. Might not help. Couldn't hurt.

"This woman's missing. Ever seen her?" he said to a woman rounding up three kids under the age of eight.

The woman looked at the photo and said, "Yes. I saw her at Good Will in Maryville. She was with a black woman."

Simon got a description of the woman and her car, exchanged

phone numbers and rushed to tell Zack.

"You won't believe this. I just met a lady whose youngest kid had a tonsillectomy at Blount Memorial. She was outside the cafeteria with her two older kids, when this friendly lady named Delta strikes up a conversation with the kids about computers. This Delta had lost her job, was living in her car and getting leftovers from the cafeteria. The lady remembered the incident because she felt sorry for Delta and offered her some money until she could get on her feet. Delta refused to take money from a woman supporting three kids."

"Is there a point to all this, Simon?"

"This lady saw Delta again at Good Will in Maryville. This time, a young lady was with Delta in an old green Lincoln with Blount County plates."

That got Zack's full attention. "And...?

"Don't you get it? Delta's the woman who stopped getting food from the cafeteria. The young lady with her was Abby."

"You were right all along. Where is she now?"

"Well, I don't know. But the description of Delta and her car gives me something to work with."

"Who would've thought? Find a clue at the zoo," Zack said.

"We need to get back to the motel, Zack. The lady also said the storm is about to hit this area."

Oliver finished at Zack's place and went to the hospital and found Minnie restless by Zelphie's bed.

"I was hoping she'd wake up before I left," Minnie said.

"She's in good hands. We need to get home."

"I know. The storm. This is all my fault for waiting so long to bring her to the hospital."

"Don't be silly. You're worse than Zack, taking on the burdens of the world," he said, opening the truck door.

"Mercy. I can't remember the last time you opened a car door for me," she said, smiling as Oliver took the wheel. "Could it be my husband missed me a little bit last night?"

"Can't a man open a door for his wife without a fuss?"

By the time they reached the mountains, rain had turned to sleet. They stopped to give Nita June a report on Zelphie.

"Then, she'll be okay?" Nita June said.

"The doctor says a little rest will do the trick. You ready for the storm?" Oliver said. "It's supposed to be bad."

"We got gas heat. We'll be warm. My husban's bringin' candles when he comes frum work. I 'magine they'll close early 'cause of the weather."

"He better get here soon. Roads are already icy."

"We've got time to run home and get some candles if you want us to," Minnie said.

"Naw. We got a kerosene lamp."

"That's good. The phones and lights will go first. Times like this, I appreciate a fireplace," Oliver said.

"Any word on Abby?" Nita June said.

"Nothing new I'm afraid," Minnie said.

They drove on and as they passed Zack's road, Minnie said, "I sure do miss Sammy."

"Zack left a phone number for the motel. Maybe you can call him before the phone goes out."

"Yes. We'll do that."

Dwight gave Delta his phone number and said goodbye at the Sunset Diner. For the first time in ages she regretted not having a phone number to give him. He said he'd be back after he won the Karaoke contest. She had no doubts he could win any contest he set his mind to.

She and Priss lingered over lunch, then had two cups of coffee while watching the soaps on the TV behind the counter. Delores, the waitress-owner, was bringing them up to date on the love affairs between characters, when a bulletin interrupted with a winter storm warning.

"Glad we left the picnic area. We could've frozen to death out there and no one would have known. Storms like this is why we're goin' south. Where's the nearest motel?" Delta said.

"Murphy, North Carolina."

"How far is that from here?"

"About twenty miles," Delores said.

"Any cheap motels there?"

"They're all cheap now. Tourist season's over," Delores said. "Murphy's a small, nice, friendly town. But, finding work there might be difficult this time of year."

"Yeah? Well, we don't want work. We need a place to stay till the storm passes, then we're going to Florida," Delta said.

"I hope you find a room," Delores said.

"If we don't, we'll just keep heading south."

"You'd better find shelter somewhere. The way this storm's moving, you won't make it to Atlanta. Which is just as well. That's no place to be in an ice storm."

Dwight will be in Atlanta, probably in a high-class hotel. We should have gone with him.

"We've got to at least try to get as far as Murphy," Delta said. "How much I owe you?"

"The cowboy took care of the bill. Good luck," Delores said. "Have you ever worked as a short order cook?"

"Why?" Delta said.

"I need one. And I've got a room out back. It's available if you don't find anything else."

"That's nice to know. Thanks," Delta said as they left.

Twenty minutes later she stopped at The Haven Inn, a small independent motel in Murphy, North Carolina. The no vacancy sign was out. According to the desk clerk the winter storm had forced travelers off the road. All motels in town were full. Delta took his word for it, since she didn't have time to look and headed back to the Sunset Diner.

The nurse called Thad when Zelphie woke up, and within thirty minutes he was in her room. Her story was not that of a deranged woman. She was deeply concerned about the consequences of revealing her knowledge.

"You were right not telling anyone before coming to me. And don't feel sorry for the people involved. They caused their own trouble," Thad said.

"Oh, I don't feel sorry for them. I feel sorry for the people who love them."

"Will you do something for me?"

"If it'll rid me of the burden and get me out of this bed."

"Can you keep this conversation between the two of us?"

"As you know, Sheriff, I'm pretty good at keeping secrets."

He laughed and shook his head. "Sometimes keeping quiet is good. Try to get better. Leave everything else to me."

He closed the door to her room behind him and found O'Dell and Anderson waiting in the hall.

"She didn't see their faces, so she can't identify the man next door as one of them," Thad said. "But she saw the car pull away from the scene shortly before the truckers arrived."

"That explains the brogan tracks leading off into the woods from the crime scene," O'Dell said. "She got a dog?"

"Does a hunter have a gun?" the sheriff said.

"If she can't identify the men, we're no better off than we were yesterday. Is that what you're saying, ah, Sheriff?" It was hard for Anderson not to call him sir when his very presence demanded authority.

"That's not what I'm saying at all, Anderson."

"She identified the car, didn't she?" O'Dell said.

"Nailed it right down to the license plate. She knows who owns the car and who runs with him. One is the guy next door."

"Then, you want us to proceed as planned," Anderson said.

"Not exactly. No one else knows she didn't see their faces. So, keep it to yourselves. Let others assume we have a witness. Here's the names of the men she thinks were in the car. Bring them in for questioning and pray Alday gains consciousness soon. Zelphie said out of the four he'd be the one to come forward and tell the truth."

Chicken Run was playing on TV and they were eating popcorn

128

when Zack's cell phone rang. He stepped through the adjoining door to Simon's room.

"You're saying that four men abducted Abby, and Zelphie knew all this time?"

"You've got to understand, Zack. . .," Thad said.

"No. You've got to understand. Abby's still missing and Zelphie had information that might have helped us find her. What are you doing about it?"

"She didn't know it was Abby. She'd never seen her. When she found out, she tried to come to me with the information. She was too sick."

"Doesn't make a bit of difference who the woman was. She should've reported it immediately and you know it."

"She knows it, too. But the woman she found was okay, and the truckers called the police. Carrying the burden has put her in the hospital. Do you want me to arrest an eighty-four-year-old woman in her hospital bed? Or concentrate on getting the men involved in the abduction? The men she identified."

"Who are these men?"

"Now, Zack. You know I can't tell you until we've picked them up for questioning."

Zack was silent, wondering how things got so complicated.

"Zack? You still there?"

"Yeah. I'm here. And, I'm mad as the dickens. You don't have to remind me of Zelphie's age. I've known her for fifteen years. And, no. I don't want you to arrest her. I'm just surprised and hurt that she didn't come to me. That's all."

"She figured if you had known who they were, you'd be in jail for murder."

"She was probably right about that."

"And, Zack. Keep this to yourself. No one needs to know what she saw or didn't see."

"I understand. Keep me informed." Zack hung up and waited to calm down. He cracked the door to his room where Simon was enjoying *Chicken Run* as much as Sammy. He caught Simon's eye and motioned for him to come.

"What's up?" Simon whispered.

"Thad thinks he's found four guys who abducted Abby. No details, yet, but he's got his hands full. Finding Abby is up to us and it's time we got serious."

"I knew finding her would be up to us and I've been serious from the beginning. You've been hiding behind a boy."

Zack's jaws clenched. "No one else could get away with that comment. But, you're right. I'll call Oliver to come get Sammy. He needs to be at home and we need to get busy."

"Did you forget why we're holding up in this motel room?"

"The storm. But it won't hit here for several hours."

"The storm will hit your place long before it gets here. Knoxville's expecting snow. Soda Creek will probably get ice."

"Right. Oliver won't have time to get Sammy, and then back home. I'll take him home, then meet you. Where will you be?"

"You'd better get a move on, if you expect to get home before the storm hits. Take care of Sammy. Let me do my job."

"You don't want my help?"

"Not in your present state of mind."

"You're probably right." *He felt strange, acting like he was as concerned for Sammy as he was about Abby. She was the one out there in trouble. What kind of monster was he?*

"You want to know what I think?" Simon said.

"Not really. But I'm sure you're going to tell me."

"You're a good man, Zack."

"Gee, thanks. Maybe you can tell the man upstairs."

"That's just the dressing. Let me finish. You're famous for sticking your neck out to help friends. I'm living proof of that. But, you don't walk on water. What you're doing now is not just helping. It's different. Think about it, Zack. What makes a man befuddled, obsessive, protective and plumb stupid?"

"You seem to have all the answers. Why don't you tell me?"

"The only thing that screws up a fellow's head like yours is right now is love, Son. Somehow, though one has nothing to do with the other, you got Abby living in your house all tangled up with finally unplugging Marie. Seems to me the doctor and Mrs. Williams made that clear."

"What made you such an expert?"

"Years of screwing up my own life."

"You're probably right. I need to tell Sammy that his mother is missing and he'll have to stay with Minnie so I can find her. What do you think about that?"

"Truth usually works best. He's a smart kid. Probably handle it better than you've been doing."

"Don't you think I've had enough scolding for one day?"

"Maybe. But, if Abby doesn't know who she is, she might not remember Sammy. He shouldn't be exposed to that. We need to find her and know her condition before bringing him into it. And you need to get a grip. When the storm lets up I'm out of here. I'll keep you informed."

The door slowly opened and Sammy's head peeked in.

"You missed *Chicken Run*," he said.

"Come here, Sammy. I want to talk to you," Zack said.

"Did I do something bad?" His forehead was lined with fear.

"No, Son." Zack pulled the boy up on his knee.

"I'll be next door if you need me. Let me know when you leave," Simon said, thinking, he had things to do. First on his list, get Delta's last name and license plate number. Then find the Lincoln, and pray the two women are still in it.

Icicles hung from the roof of Nita June's trailer. The salesman had called it a Mobile home. Whatever it was called, strong winds whipping against it, shook the foundation like it would blow away any minute.

The boys were in bed and the kerosene lamp was filled and ready to use, if the lights went out. Nita June sat by the window sipping coffee, praying her husband hadn't had a wreck. She was also dealing with old fears, hoping he wasn't drinking on a night like this. Suddenly, she heard a crash and pulled back the curtain. Her husband's truck had slammed against a tree. She watched him get out, fight the wind, stagger to the door. He was drunk. Her fears had become reality. She took a deep breath. Maybe she should lock him out. She knew she couldn't. Not in a storm like this. Besides, he'd just break down the door and they'd all freeze to death.

He pushed in, cursing, knocking over a chair.

Nita June struggled to close the door against the strong wind behind him. "Where have you been?"

"You know better 'n to ask me that, woman."

"I wuz worried you might'a had a wreck. Did ya' have trouble on the road?"

"I had trouble all right. But not on the road. The stupid police wuz nosing 'round my job. Ain't that against the law?"

"Police? What did they want?"

"They wuz askin' about a lost woman and a man trying to hang himself. They pick on hard working folks like me, when they ought to go after the rich man. He brought her here."

"Rich man? You mean Abby. Why'd they ask you about her?"

"Didn't think I knowed you been hanging 'round her, did you? Hopin' some of that rich man's money'd rub off on you. You can't hide things frum me. When 'er you gonna learn that? I know what goes on 'round here."

"What man tried to hang himself?"

"Some blabber-mouth."

His slurry speech and know-it-all attitude made her sick to her stomach. He stumbled and knocked a picture from the wall. Glass splattered all over the floor.

"Whur's Frank? Git that boy in here to clean up this mess."

"Frank's in bed. Leave him alone."

Soon the storm in the trailer was as bad as the one outside. A nightmare, repeating itself. Only this time was worse than the others. The front room was a wreck. Her body was bruised and bloody. She had to keep him occupied, out of the boy's room. *God, let him pass out. I can't take much more.* She waited for the right moment. Bam. She hit him in the head with an iron skillet. He fell to the floor.

Run. Go outside. Too cold. Can't leave the boys. The boys. She took a gun from the wall, fumbled in the drawer for bullets, then ran to their room and locked the door.

"Frank. Git under the bed with Billy. Be very quiet."

She stood against the door and waited.

Maybe he'll stay unconscious. What if I've killed him?

She jumped as he banged against the door.

"Open up," he said.

"Go away. This gun's loaded and aimed at the door."

"Stupid witch. You can't keep me out if I want to get in. You ain't got the guts to shoot me. I'm ya' husband."

Wham. He broke the door open.

"Please. Don't make me shoot you," she cried.

"Where's Frank?"

He looked in the closet and started for the bed. Nita June pushed him away. He turned and slapped her so hard she bounced against the wall and fell.

"I'll shoot. I won't let you hurt Frank anymore."

He knelt, reached under the bed, grabbed Frank's leg and pulled him out.

"You know better than to hide from me, boy," he said, and smacked Frank's face hard enough to break his jaw.

Nita June slapped the gun across his back as hard as she could. He let go of Frank and lunged for her. He pushed her back over a chair. His hands were around her neck, choking her. The chair tilted over. They fell to the floor.

Boom. The gun went off.

Chapter Eighteen

"It's small. Only a peephole of a window and no view. But it's got twin beds and you'll be safe from the storm," Delores said, showing the room to Delta.

"Anything's better than nothing. How much are you asking?"

"Are you taking the cook's job?" Delores said.

"I weren't planning to stay that long. And, I'm a computer tech, not a cook. Does the room come with the job?"

"Sort of."

They discussed the price of the room if they only stayed through the storm, versus taking the job and staying longer. They finally settled. The room was free, with the job. Delores was about to leave when Priss curled up on the bed and groaned.

"Is she okay?" Delores said.

"Must be coming down with something. I think I've got some aspirins in the car."

"Well, if you don't, I've got some in the diner."

"I'll be over in a few minutes for you to show me around."

"No hurry. I won't have business till the storm passes."

Delta held the rails that led to the car where snow already covered the hood. Unable to find aspirins, she went back in the room, took the covers off her bed and spread them over Priss.

"Don't go getting sick on me, Priss. And, don't take your shoes off. We'll probably be leaving once the customers taste my cooking. Lord. Why did I take this job when I can't cook?"

"I can cook. But not as good as him," Priss said.

"How good is your cooking?"

No answer.

"A man who cooks can't be all bad. Is he the same man who told you to stay on the bench under the streetlight?"

Priss didn't answer. The bed felt good. Warm at last, she closed her eyes.

Delta headed to the diner, hoping Priss would stay put. She didn't want to find her gone, sitting under a streetlight waiting for him, whoever him is? So Priss can cook. Will wonders never cease? Maybe Priss should take the cook's job. Come to think of it, she didn't tell Delores she could cook. Since the woman was good to her, saved her from the storm and all, she decided to level on the cooking business.

"Before I sign on this deal, I think you should know. I'm not much of a cook," she said, following Delores to the kitchen.

"Awe, anybody can flip burgers and bacon. I'll cook main meals until you learn the ropes." Delores showed her where to find things and explained procedures.

"This doesn't seem too hard. Priss is a good cook. Maybe I can manage until she gets better," Delta said.

Well, she says she can cook I believe her. She said she could drive, then drove off and left my butt.

"That's all there is to it. If the electricity goes off, there's some candles on the table and a few books by the bed."

"What kind of books?"

"A variety of paperbacks."

"I need those aspirins. I couldn't find mine."

"If you ever feel like talking, I've got big shoulders," Delores said and gave Delta a bottle of aspirins.

"You live around here?"

"I've got an apartment above the diner."

"That's real handy," Delta said and went to her room.

She scanned the TV channels. Nothing interesting. She turned the sound down, left it on the weather channel, and took the books from the drawer. Mysteries and romance. She chose a mystery. Before she started reading, she got up and felt Priss's forehead. Was she hot from fever, or too much cover?

Nina June lay still a few seconds, staring in shock at her lifeless husband on the floor with a hole in his chest. Frank was sitting on the bed, holding the gun. Billy was playing peek-a-boo from under the bed like it was a big game.

"Frank. Honey, gimme the gun and git back under the bed with Billy. Stay 'till I call you." She covered her husband's bloody body with a blanket from the closet. "Okay. You can come out now." She squeezed her sons. "I'm sorry. So sorry."

Frank's face was blank. Billy grinned and said, "Boo."

She led them to her bedroom near the front of the trailer.

"You can sleep in my bed tonight. I'll be in the living' room for a while."

"Will you sleep with us, Mama?" Frank said.

"Yes, I will. First, I need t' call the police."

"Will they take us to jail?"

"Lord, no, Son. Ever'thing's gonna be fine."

After tucking them in, she closed the bedroom door and went to the living room. She sat down on the couch. Her bloody hands trembled as she picked up the phone. No dial tone. She cried and prayed. *Lord God. Help me. Please. Help me.*

The lights blinked, then went out. From the flickering gas heater, she could see well enough to find the lamp. Her shaking hands removed the glass shade and lit the wick. She stood frozen, watching shadows bounce against the wall. Finally she sat down on a chair and rocked back and forth. With her face in her hands, she cried until she could hardly breathe.

Bam. Bam. Bam.

She jumped. Was someone at the door, or was it the wind? Maybe someone heard the gun shot. Not knowing what to expect, she moved slowly across the room, opened the door and stared at Pete O'Dell and a female officer she didn't know.

"Nita, this is Deputy Anderson," O'Dell said, noticing the bruises and blood on Nita June's face and clothes. He'd known her since high school. He also knew about her marital problems.

"Can we come in?" he said, cautiously looking around.

136

She grabbed him in a bear hug. "Thank God you're here. How did you know?"

"Know what, Mam?" Anderson said, standing erect with her arms folded on her chest. "What's going on here?"

"Back off, Anderson," O'Dell said.

"I tried to call. The phone's out." Using her shirtsleeve, Nita June smeared bloody tears across her face.

"We didn't know anything was wrong, Nita. We came to talk to Jess," O'Dell said.

"He's in the back room. I think he's dead."

When Zack stopped at the service station on the way home, Sammy sat still, watching his every move, not restless like most kids his age.

He had almost waited too late to start home. Ice was forming on the road. He would never make it up the mountain without chains on the tires. Sammy didn't understand, so Zack took him from the car and explained as he put the chains on before driving slowly up the steep, slick, mountain road.

He pressed the automatic garage door opener on the sun-visor. "Good. The electricity's still on."

Once inside, he made hot vegetable soup and set up trays in front of the fireplace. Sammy dumped a handful of oyster crackers in his bowl and soon wanted a second helping.

"Are you going to leave me and find Mommy when I go to sleep?" Sammy said, his eyelids getting droopy.

"Not tonight. I'll wait until the weather clears up so Oliver and Minnie can come get you."

"Will you sleep in my room with me tonight?"

"I have an idea. Let's get quilts and pillows and sleep in front of the fireplace."

"That's a dandy idea," the boy said, a phrase he had picked up from Oliver. "Like camping out, only camping in."

When Sammy was warm and cozy, he fell asleep. Zack went to his office and called Oliver.

"I finally told Sammy that his mother is lost and he'll be staying with you while I go find her," he said.

"He had no trouble with that?" Oliver said.

"Not a bit. He was down-right excited."

"Minnie will be, too. You gained his trust by phoning him while you were away in Denver. That made a big difference."

"And, he's gotten to know you and Minnie."

"Well, that too. But, I'll tell you something, Zack. He's smarter than we give him credit for. He probably already knew his mother was missing," Oliver said.

"You think so?"

"He's very astute. I'll say that. By the way, I lit the heater in the green house to protect the Meidilands, and filled the generator. You'll be needing it in a few hours. Ice is already forming. They say the storm will be gone in a couple of days. I think it'll stall on the mountains as usual and we'll be stranded in below zero temperatures for a long time."

"For once, I hope they're right and you're wrong. I'll be in touch when I'm ready to leave," Zack said.

"I don't think you'll be leaving any time soon."

Zack was talking to Dennis at the Chicago office when the line went dead and the lights went off. He settled in front of the fire and lay awake listening to trees breaking from the weight of ice, like shotguns going off around the house.

With no electricity, no phone, locked away from the world outside, he had time to think. Perhaps because of Simon's lecture he was realizing, or admitting to himself, that his feelings for Abby ran much deeper than just friends.

When the guard first called Thad and said Zelphie wanted to visit Larry Alday, Thad said no. After the third call, he gave in. She had a strange sense about her and would probably talk the man into consciousness.

She was sitting by Larry's bed talking to him when he opened his eyes. Her face was the first thing he saw.

"Do you know who I am?" she said.

"You're Zelphie, the ghost lady who walks the mountains. They say you're crazy. I never believed it, though I've always been a little scared of you." His voice was rasp and weak, his throat sore. "Where am I?"

"You're in the Clearwater hospital."

"I thought I might have made it to Heaven, with the white sheets and all."

"Except for the Grace of God you would be."

"God might not want me in Heaven, after what I did."

"What did you do?"

With a shaky, hoarse voice, he told his story.

"If that's true, you did no wrong. I've known you all your life. Your Ma and Pa before you. You're a good boy."

"I didn't go along with it, but I didn't stop them."

"Could you have stopped them if you had tried?"

"I tried. I begged them not to hurt her. I didn't want to leave her. But when I went back and found the police there, I didn't have the courage to stop. And, I didn't have the guts to turn myself in, cause I was scared to tell on the others. I kept hearing a voice inside from my childhood saying don't be a tattletale. In my heart, I knew what I had to do. Somehow, I thought I could get the others to turn themselves in with me."

"So, you went back and checked on the girl. What would you have done if the police hadn't been there?"

"I wouldn't have left her in the woods. 'Course, I couldn't have taken her home. I didn't know who she was, or where she lived. She seemed sick, so I probably would have taken her to the hospital."

"She was sick. At heart. Her little boy had been bitten by a copperhead. She thought he was dead."

"Lord help us. We should have been helping and we were hurting."

"None of you knew who she was?"

"Jess said something that made me think he knew. Then I heard the neighbors talking about the picture on the pamphlets around town. That's when I tried to get the others to go to the police. They called me a religious nut. Said I preached too much about God and ghosts and goblins. When I threatened to go to the police, they did this. You know what, Zelphie? I forgot to ask for God's guidance in handling the problem," he said, reaching his hand up, touching the rope burns on his neck.

"What made ya'll leave the girl in the woods when you did?"

"We heard a noise."

"How about that? God puts people in the oddest places at the strangest times."

"It was you, weren't it?" He smiled. "You're a good ghost, Zelphie. But God will surely punish me for not fighting harder for that poor girl."

"Maybe God doesn't have punishment in mind. Maybe he's planning to use you."

"Do you really think so? After all I've done?"

"Could be why he left you here. By all rights you should be dead. God doesn't make mistakes, Larry. Why don't you start searching for your mission? Ask His help in your decision."

"I already know my mission, Zelphie. I just don't know how to go about it."

"If the plan is clear in your head, God will show you the way. First, you've got to tell the sheriff everything you've told me. It's not squealing. It's doing what's right."

She handed him a Holy Bible and left the room.

"Call the sheriff," she told the policeman in the hallway. "Tell him the man's awake and wants to talk."

Chapter Nineteen

After O'Dell signed off the radio with Thad, he pushed against the wind, making his way back to the trailer. Once inside, he stood by the heater warming his near-frozen hands, while he repeated the conversation to Anderson.

She plopped down on the couch, legs sprawled in front, hands folded on her belly. "So. We're stranded in this trailer with a woman, two kids, and a dead man."

"Yep," O'Dell said.

"Are they sending an ambulance?"

O'Dell laughed. "On icy, mountain roads? Not hardly. When this dad-burned storm finishes whatever it's going to do, the county road crew will clear the main roads. The back roads, where we are, will be cleared last. From what I saw out there in the dark, everything is covered with ice. Trees are breaking from the weight and falling on electric wires. Some of the poles are broken. It'll take a hundred electricians, chain saws, bulldozers, and God knows what else to get us out of here. Unless you want to walk twenty miles on ice, we're in here for the long haul."

"And to think I left the sunshine state to work in the beautiful Tennessee mountains where life is still simple and good. What do we do now?"

"Get the body bag from the car. We've got to put Jess outside on the ice."

"What?"

"Do you know what the warm temperature in this trailer will do to a corpse? We bag him and put him out where it's probably ten to twenty below zero. That's the only way."

"Doesn't the medical examiner have to get here first?"

"In this case, we're the medical examiners."

"We should've waited 'til after the storm to come question Jess. We really made a bad call, didn't we?"

"Not the way I see it. Either way, Jess wouldn't be here to question." O'Dell sat down in the chair. He shouldn't feel sorry for his rookie partner. This was good training. "Do you believe in fate, Anderson?"

"Don't tell me you think all this is fate."

"Imagine what would have happened here if we hadn't showed up when we did. No phone. No lights. No way to get help and a dead man in the bedroom."

"When you put it that way…"

"Let's get busy. If we're lucky, we can catch thirty winks before daylight. There'll be plenty to do tomorrow."

"I thought it was forty winks," Anderson joked, looked up and saw Nita June standing in the hallway door holding blankets and pillows. Her brown, curly hair stuck out all over the place. Her big hazel eyes were swollen. She hadn't cleaned the blood from her split lip. She looked like a punching bag.

"This is all I got, 'cept what's on the boys," she said.

"Give us a pillow and go to bed, Nita," O'Dell said.

She gave them a pillow and tears started streaming down her face. O'Dell put his hand on her shoulder.

"I'm sorry. I don't use'ly act like this," she said.

O'Dell put his arms around her. Anderson had gotten to her feet and was looking like her heart would break. "No need to apologize. Not after what's happened here tonight."

"It'll all work out," O'Dell said, and looked at Anderson. "Fate. Pure and simple fate."

"I see what you mean," Anderson said, cleared her throat and went out in the blizzard to get the body bag. *Nothing like this could ever happen in Florida.*

Delta woke up and took another shower. She couldn't remember feeling so clean. Leaving Priss in bed, she went to the diner to see if she could rustle up something to eat.

Delores was making coffee. "Is Priss better?"

"I think she's worse. She's in bed, staring into space."

"You must be hungry," Delores said.

"I could eat a horse."

"Don't have horses. Got pigs and chickens," Delores said. "Unless you're a health nut. In which case I've got cereal. Hot and cold."

"Right now I'll eat anything that doesn't eat me first."

"Then, bacon and eggs it is."

"I might as well show you what I can do in the kitchen," Delta said, put on an apron and went to the grill.

"The grill has to warm up first. Is Priss coming?"

"I'll go get her when breakfast is ready," Delta said.

"Why do you have to go get her?"

"How long before this grill's hot enough to cook on?" Delta said, hoping her new friend would stop asking questions.

Delores filled their cups with coffee. "What's with her?"

"I'm not sure," Delta said.

"Is she kin?"

Delta grinned and said, "Do we look like kin?"

"Oh, you mean the skin thing. You probably wouldn't pass as sisters. But, she depends on you, you're protective of her."

Delta hesitated, then decided to get an objective opinion.

"I don't even know her name. What's worse, *she* doesn't know her name, where she's from, nothing. I named her Priss."

"My God," Delores said, wondering if she should just keep her mouth shut. Maybe she ought to help them on their way to Florida. Curiosity got the best of her. "You mean she doesn't know who she is?"

"Nope. I found her in a hospital gown, hunkered down under a bridge."

Delta took a stool on the customer side of the bar.

"Why didn't you take her to a hospital, or to the police?"

"Apparently you've never been through the legal system."

"You're not running from the law, are you?"

"God, no. I'm not. Like I said, I don't know about her. I felt sorry for her. She was half naked. I found her some clothes to put on and started looking after her. She wouldn't have lasted a week on the streets alone."

Delores poured more coffee, tossed bacon on the grill, and listened. When Delta got to the part where Priss drove off and left her, Delores threw back her head and roared.

"I was walking when Dwight came along and gave me a lift."

"You just met him? Lord, I thought ya'll were a couple."

"Don't I wish? Anyway, we found my car out of gas beside the road like I knew we would, and Priss was sitting on a bench under a street light," Delta said.

"Mercy. Didn't it occur to you that she might have loved ones worried to death, looking for her?"

"I figured if anybody cared about her, she couldn't have been where I found her."

"What are you going to do?"

"I'm gonna take care of her, help her get her memory back. I think she's starting to remember. Like when Dwight and I found her, she said a man told her to wait under a streetlight while he went to get something. I thought she was talking about a pimp for sure. No way I was turning that sweet thing back into something like that. When she said the man could cook and she hadn't just met him, I figured she was remembering, talking about somebody from her past. Besides, pimps can't cook."

"How do you know pimps can't cook?"

"I just came to that on my own," Delta said.

"Can't you be charged with kidnapping if you take her across state lines from Tennessee to Florida? My Lord. What if she's running from the mob and they get after you?" Delores scooped food from the grill to the plates.

"Hadn't thought about that."

"If I were you, I'd sure as heck be thinking about it," Delores said. *Maybe, now that you've told me, I'm as guilty as you. Maybe*

I'm harboring fugitives. "Lord have mercy. We'd better keep this to ourselves until you figure out what to do. Food's ready. Go get Priss and let's eat."

"See how great I am in the kitchen? Looks good. I'll be right back."

In a few minutes, she returned, sat down, and started eating.

"Where's Priss?"

"She's not coming. You think the road to Murphy is clear?"

"Should be. The storm wasn't that bad here."

"Soon as I finish eating, I'm taking her to a doctor."

"What are you going to tell him? You'll need a last name."

"Yeah? Well, now, according to you, I can give her my last name. Tell him we're sisters."

"I'll give you the name and address of my doctor friend in Murphy. He's always busy, so he'll probably have to work you in. Tell him I sent you, that Priss works for me."

Zack got up, added wood to the fire, and laid back down on the pallet beside Sammy. Sometime in the wee hours of the morning, after the wind subsided, he fell asleep.

At daylight he got up and put on his heavy coat and gloves. He was hoping Sammy would sleep another hour while he checked on the condition outside.

The wind had blown from the east so that the front doors were frozen shut with three feet of snow over an inch of ice that ran to the edge of the porch. The back door was frozen shut too, but he finally got it open. The snow was so deep, he couldn't tell where the porch ended. He plodded across the yard in snow still falling so thick he couldn't see five feet ahead.

"This is something," Oliver said, coming up the driveway.

"Let's go down the mountain and assess the damage."

"Just got back. Broken trees are tangled in telephone and electric wires across the road all the way down. Light poles are broken. It'll take days with chain saws to clean it up."

"How's your road?"

"Better than yours. My thermometer said fifteen below."

"We need to hire some help."

"How, Zack? The phones are out. I heard on my CB radio, all of Soda Creek is like this."

"Boy! What a mess. Let's take Sammy to Minnie, and get started," Zack said as they headed back toward his house. "Come in. I'll make coffee on the fireplace."

"Naw. I'll go tell Minnie Sammy's coming and get the chain saw ready."

Zack went in the garage and got the ten inch portable TV-radio. When he opened the back door, Sammy was running through the house calling his name.

"I'm here, Sammy. I got the TV from the garage. After breakfast, we'll go to Oliver's house."

Sammy grabbed Zack's legs with tears streaming down his face. "I thought you'd left me."

"No, Son. Not in a million years," Zack said.

Simon spent the day on the phone and the Internet. He was unable to find what he needed most, Delta's last name. All he had was a description of Delta and her car, an old, green Lincoln Continental with a Blount county, Tennessee tag.

The weather report said the worst of the storm had hit the mountains where Zack lived. He dialed Zack's number. The phone was out of order. The State Police said the main road was clear south of Maryville.

He checked out of the motel and headed south on Highway 129. If a person was going south and had no money for motel rooms, they would avoid Interstates and stick to back roads. No police, no hassle. Since Delta had a car, she must have decided to go to a warmer climate for the winter. Maybe for good. Why and how did she connect with Abby? Did she abduct Abby from the hospital? If so, why? If Abby wasn't abducted, why would she go? Of course! She had lost her memory. Apparently she hadn't found it.

He thought the roads would be crowded after the storm. He was wrong. They were desolate. His gas gauge was almost on empty and he was past hungry. He had missed breakfast and lunch and he hadn't seen a restaurant for miles.

Like a lighthouse in a storm he saw what appeared to be a truck-stop diner up ahead. It could be a greasy spoon for all he cared. He had Tums and Zantac. With luck, the waitress would be a knockout. He would dazzle her with his charm, ask about Abby, get information on a motel, and whatever else she cared to share with him.

He pulled in, filled up the tank, and then moved his car to the side next to a brown SUV. A black eighteen-wheeler sat next to the diesel pump. No one was in sight. He got out of his Caddy, grabbed his briefcase and headed in the diner. Overhead, a sign said: "Welcome to the Sunset Diner."

Chapter Twenty

He sat at a table in the corner and analyzed the six customers. The four in the booth belonged to the SUV. The two men at the right end of the bar drove the eighteen-wheeler. He got up and moved to the opposite end of the bar so he could see the door.

"Hi. I'm Delores. I'll be your waitress."

"Nice to meet you, Delores. I'm Simon. I'll be your favorite customer."

The tall, slender, blond waitress smiled and put a glass of water, a menu, and silverware on the counter in front of him.

"The dinner special is listed on the board," she said.

"Looks like you missed the ice and snow," Simon said.

"No ice. Got enough snow to take a day off. I hear the worst hit the east Tennessee Mountains before it got here."

"You heard right. They got the ice. I've been unable to contact my friend in that area for a couple of days."

"Want a minute to read the menu?"

"The special sounds good to me. Fried chicken, mashed potatoes and gravy, peas, cornbread, sweet iced tea."

Simon watched Delores go to the kitchen. She was wearing tight jeans and a red T-shirt. No wedding ring. With her looks maybe she had someone in the wings. Maybe not. Maybe she was between relationships, like him. Maybe he'd find out. A lot of maybe's. He took Abby's photo from his briefcase, and then put it back. Best to get acquainted before explaining his mission.

She put his food and tea on the bar.

"You here for business or pleasure?"

"Little of both."

When he started eating, she left to serve new customers in the corner booth, then returned.

"Is the road clear to Asheville?" she said.

"Don't know. I came 129 from Maryville."

She turned away, wiped the counter that didn't need cleaning and knocked over the saltshaker.

Is it my imagination, or is my charming personality and good looks making her nervous?

"Could I have more water?" he said, wanting her to turn around so he could see her face.

She poured water and turned her back before speaking.

"So, you're from Maryville?"

"I'm from Nashville. Business took me to Maryville, then brought me here. I guess the nearest motel is in Murphy."

"You guess right. How long will you be in Murphy?"

She had opened the conversation door. Ordinarily, he would step in. He would wait, examine that possibility later.

"Probably overnight," he said, waiting to see if her nervous condition continued.

She went to the kitchen, and then returned. He watched as she nibbled his bait. She didn't want to appear too obvious.

"How was the food?" she asked, as he pushed his plate back.

"Best I've had lately."

"I got peach cobbler, lemon pie, and chocolate cake."

"I'll take the cobbler. With ice cream."

"Good choice," she said, scooped up a dish of cobbler and ice cream, and dropped it on the way to the counter.

"Do I make you nervous?"

"Now wouldn't that be nice?" she said, half smiled, stepped over the mess and scooped out another dish of cobbler.

"What time do you close?"

"Usually around eleven. It depends on the customers," she said and started cleaning up her mess. She told the young man wearing an apron to catch two new customers.

The dinner crowd was gathering. He had to make a move. He

149

opened his briefcase and pulled out Abby's picture.

"Ever seen this woman?"

Delores looked at the photo and dropped the plate of food she was holding.

Reactions. Expressions. Worth a million words!

"I'm not sure. Lots of people come through here. She's real pretty. Who is she?"

"She's my friend's fiancé." *Not exactly true, but if his guess was right, she would be if he could find her.*

"Why are you looking for her if she's his fiancé?"

"I'm a detective," he said.

She squatted behind the bar to clean up the broken plate.

"You don't look like a policeman."

"Private."

"Got any proof, Mr. P.I.?"

Simon flashed his ID.

"Is this girl in some kind of trouble with the law? Or is her fiancé just checking up on her?"

"I can't divulge that information. But she's definitely not a criminal. In fact, she may be in danger."

"Hmm. Can you leave her photo with me? I'll post it and be on the lookout."

"Sure. No problem," he said.

"Has this gal got a name?"

"Abby Crowley," he said, and put his business card and the photo on the counter. "If you see her before I get back, I'd appreciate a call."

"You're coming back this way?" she said, dumping the broken dish in the garbage and picking up his card.

"That's the plan. Should be back in a day or two. Maybe then you and I can have a cup of coffee and get acquainted," he said, pushed back his broad shoulders and stood up.

"I'm kinda tied up at the moment," she said. *Liar, liar. Pants on fire. Here stands a six-foot-two hunk, taller than you for a change, sinfully handsome, with a beard you'd like to feel next to your cheek. His brown bedroom eyes knocks your socks off, and you're turning him away to protect two women you hardly know, who may not even need protecting.*

"Any chance you'll get untied?" He grinned and picked up his briefcase.

"We'll see." She went to clear the bar where the truckers had been sitting.

"See you, Delores," Simon said, and headed for the door.

I'll be back. Vibes are too strong to ignore—business and pleasure wise. How lucky is that?

Thirty minutes later he checked into a Best Western on the outskirts of Murphy, across the street from a steak house and a Wal-mart Super Center. He tossed his briefcase on the bed and dialed Zack's number. Still out of order. He left the motel and drove around scanning motel parking lots, though he was almost certain Delta wouldn't be in a motel. He looked in parks, under bridges, and then went back to his room. Tomorrow, he'd check the hospital and talk to the local police. He turned on the TV, but his mind was on the Sunset Diner. Something was going on there besides serving food. Perhaps he should have hid and watched the diner instead of coming to Murphy. That's what he'd do tomorrow if he didn't find anything here. A weather report flashed on the screen and he turned up the volume. A tornado-like ice storm had demolished a twenty-mile radius of the Cherokee National Forest around Soda Creek. An old man was saying he had lived there all his life and had never seen anything like it. The cameras moved to working crews clearing away fallen trees tangled in electric wires that was blocking Highway 68 close to Zack's road.

He smiled. He wouldn't be bothered with his friend's help for a while. Right about now, a few miles over the mountains as the crow flies, Zack was a lumberjack with a chain saw.

After working six hours, only stopping to warm up with hot coffee from the thermos, they had barely made a dent in the mess across the road. It was still below zero. Zack's older partner had slowed down considerably.

"Let's call it quits," Zack said.

"Are you sure?" Oliver said.

"This'll take several days no matter how hard we work."

"All right then." Oliver started gathering the equipment.

"I think I'll walk down to the highway and see if anybody has a working phone so I can call Simon. It's only a couple of miles," Zack said, thinking of peace and warmth in the church.

"Okay. We'll stop and check on Nita June," Oliver said.

"What's this 'we' business?"

"I thought I'd go with you."

"You need to go see if Minnie and Sammy are okay and let them know we're alive."

"Okay. If you're not back by dark, I'm coming to look for you," Oliver said. "Don't forget to check on Nita June."

"Sure thing," Zack said and started out through deep snow, thinking electric heat was no good in this weather. Yet, that's what most people had in the area. Who could have known? This was a rare storm. He had never seen anything like it.

The few neighbors he talked to had gas heat or fireplaces. Their phones and electricity were still out. He passed several new houses under construction. Soda Creek was growing fast and he wasn't sure that was good. Newcomers moved in because of the simple, quiet life, then immediately tried to change what they liked by pouring concrete on everything.

He crossed Highway 68 and approached the church. A deacon, who lived nearby, came from the basement.

"Hello, Brother Cole. What brings you this far on foot?"

"I'm assessing the situation. Looking for a phone."

"The phone's still out, but I've had the gas heat on all day, in case somebody shows up seeking shelter."

"Any word on when they'll have the power and phones on?"

"It may take a week or more. They say the entire south end of Monroe County is like this, all the way to High Plains. They're concentrating on clearing Highway 68 so the Care Wagon can get to the churches. It came by here this morning."

"I'm surprised the Care Wagon got here."

"I am, too. There's a shelter for desperate people at the community center in High Plains."

"Is everyone safe in our area?"

"Only one family inside. They're not members. But we never turn away those in need. Unfortunately, they showed up after the Care Wagon had gone. Go on in. I'll be in directly."

A man, woman and three small children wearing thin coats and summer shoes were huddled around the heater. Two huge trees had fallen on their house. They had no heat and no way to cook.

The deacon returned with a tray of sandwiches, hot soup and cocoa for the family. "This should warm you up."

He walked with Zack to the back of the church.

"They can stay at my place. There's plenty of room," Zack said. "I'm cooking on the fireplace."

"That's neighborly of you, Brother Cole. But they're not dressed for a two-mile hike to your place in below zero weather. They'll be fine here tonight. I expect the Care wagon will be here again in the morning. Have they found Sister Abby?"

"Not yet."

"We're all praying. They'll find her soon."

Zack left with a heavy heart. Remembering he had promised to check on Nita June, he walked over the ridge. He approached her mobile home and saw a squad car in the yard.

Through the window Nita June saw a man struggling to walk in thigh-deep snow, climbing over fallen trees and electric wires. He had on so many clothes she couldn't tell who he was. After talking to the deputies, he turned away, leaned on a broken tree, and bowed his head. Then he got in the squad car and talked on the radio. When he started toward the trailer, she recognized him. Zack.

How can I face him? He'll probably hate me. She bit her lip and opened the door. With watery eyes she said, "I didn't know, Zack. I'm so sorry."

"Me, too," he said, and embraced her.

"My husband. . ." she started.

"The deputies told me everything. If you need to get away from here, you're welcome to stay at my place. O'Dell said it would be okay. I got lots of room."

"We're fine, Zack. The trailer's warm and we have food."

"I talked to the sheriff on the radio. He's hiring me a crew. By morning, I'll have help. He said they should have you and the deputies out of here tomorrow night. Employees from the county, electric, phone company and hundreds of volunteers are working round the clock in ten below zero weather."

"Any word on Abby?" she said.

"Not yet. I just hope she's not out in this mess. Though I don't see how, and I'm sure at this point you don't either, we've got to believe that somehow there's good in all this."

With a tired body and soul, Zack headed home. He had looked for comfort and found peace in neighbors helping neighbors. He had visited a friend to offer help and found Abby's abductor, dead. With sadness, yet a peace he couldn't explain, he understood Abby's bond to Nina June.

Chapter Twenty-One

Delores was about to close the diner when Delta walked in.

"How's Priss?" Delores said.

"She's got pneumonia."

"Is she in the room?"

"She's in the Murphy hospital. I gave her my last name and all went well until I had to sign a form. They gave me a real weird look. That's when I gave Priss your last name, and said you'd be responsible for the bill. Course you can deduct it from my salary."

"Good Heavens. Now she's my sister. I hope she doesn't walk off again," Delores said.

"At the moment, she's too weak to stand up. I don't think she'll be going anywhere for a few days."

"That's the least of our worries right now," Delores said. "Put on this apron and help me clean up. As soon as that couple leaves we're having a serious conversation."

"What's up?"

Delores gave her a hard look and she said, "Okay."

The couple took their time eating. The woman was sipping beer, like it was wine, as if there was no tomorrow. The man drank coffee. Designated driver, no doubt.

Finally, Delores got tired of waiting and gave them the ticket. "I hate to rush you, but it's past our closing time."

They apologized and left.

Delores reached under the counter and pulled out Abby's photo and plopped it on the counter.

"Take a look at this. Priss is Abby Crowley. A private investigator named Simon Freely is looking for her."

"What's she wanted for?"

"Nothing. Her fiancé hired the P.I. to find her."

"Hmm…how much did you tell him?"

"As little as possible."

"What else did he say?"

"He couldn't say anything else without violating ethics or something. He left his business card. I'm supposed to call him if I see her. I'm scared, Delta."

"Yeah? Well, there's no reason to be scared. You're not going to see her. She's not here. You simply don't call him. What kind of a dude is this Simon?"

"One I'd have latched onto in a North Carolina second if I hadn't been afraid I was harboring a fugitive."

"Then he's a decent guy."

"You think I'd want to latch on to one who isn't?"

"Maybe this ain't such a bad thing. We'll trick this Simon into telling us about Priss, or Abby. Come to think of it, she looks like an Abby. Anyhow, if I can get enough information from him, I might be able to help Priss get her memory back. That is, if we get a chance to talk to him again."

"We'll get a chance. He's in Murphy, coming back in a couple of days."

"By the time he gets back, I'll be ready," Delta said.

"Be ready?"

"I mean, I'll know how to handle him."

"Simon ain't some dummy you can just handle. He's a pro from the word go. I'm sure he saw right through me. I was already nervous because he was so darn good looking. Like, the man I've waited for all my life. Then, he mentioned Maryville, said he was in this area looking for Priss, or Abby, or whatever her name is. I put on a real show, dropping dishes right and left. He asked all the right questions to make me say all the wrong answers. He even asked if he made me nervous. He'll be back. You can bet on that."

"Yeah? Well, he won't find her. She ain't here," Delta said. "Besides, he doesn't know she's with me."

"I wouldn't be too sure about that either. He tracked her here, didn't he? He's a professional, I tell you. We'll only know what he wants us to know."

"If this smart aleck knows so much, he knows I'm only trying to help her get her memory back."

"Maybe you should leave that to doctors who are trained to deal with people like Priss, or Abby. As it is, we may be just a hair above breaking the law."

"Yeah? Well, leave Simon to me. I'll handle his wagon."

Thad believed Larry's story. He'd never seen a more remorseful man. Definitely no threat to society.

"Please let me talk to Zelphie before you take me away. Put handcuffs on me, do anything. Just let me see her."

"No need for handcuffs, Larry. I'll be right back."

He knocked on Zelphie's door, and then peeked in. She was sitting in a chair looking out the window.

"You feeling well today, Zelphie?"

"Of course I am. Can't you see that? What are you gonna do with that boy next door?"

Thad stepped into the room. "He's not a boy, Zelphie. I thought you might like to see him before we take him to jail."

"Why on earth are you taking him to jail?"

"You believe I'm a good sheriff?"

"I voted for you."

"Then, leave the law to me. Okay?"

"But, he's more innocent than I am."

"That wouldn't surprise me a bit," Thad said.

"I have a right to know what's gonna happen to him."

"He'll probably be released in a week or so."

"And what about the other boys? I know about Jess. But the other two."

"They've been cooperative and will have their day in court. Probably do time. Now, do you want to talk to Larry or not?"

"Well, of course I do." She got up, took Thad's arm and slowly walked to Larry's room.

She told him he had done the right thing, even though it almost cost his life. He had been spared to do God's will. Larry said he was ashamed of what he had done. He didn't know why God would want to have anything to do with him.

"The Lord has plans for you. Trust me," Zelphie said.

"I do trust you, Zelphie. I already know what I've got to do. I have to face punishment from the law and pay for my crime. Then I have to repent my sins and serve. That's what the Lord wants me to do. I'm more sure of that than I've ever been of anything. I know He will show me how."

"Goodbye, Larry. I've got a feeling I'll see you again real soon," Zelphie said.

There was a glow about Larry, a smile on his face, and Zelphie's Bible in his hand. The deputy pulled his arms behind his back, snapped on the cuffs and led him from the room.

"Okay, Thad. When are you letting me out of this joint?"

Thad chuckled and shook his head. *Eighty-four-year-old spunk. Had to be a handful in her younger days. Still is. Another week in here and she'll be running the hospital.*

"As soon as the road to your house is clear. Or do you want to go handle that, too?"

"Looks like they could use some handling. They've been piddling around up there for days."

"Sit tight, Zelphie. You'll be back walking the mountains soon enough."

"Easy for you to say. You're not cooped up in here."

"Always got to have the last word."

"Any word I say could be my last," she said and headed for the nurses station.

Zack was bundled up and ready for another day working in zero temperature. He stepped out on the porch in the bright sun and heard the crew's chain saws working. As soon as they got his road cleared, he would go to town and call Simon.

Leaving Sammy had not been a problem once he explained why he had to leave each day. After a night on the pallet in front of the fire, the boy would get dressed, actually looking forward to spending the day with Minnie.

"I guess you'll be leaving in the morning if they get the road cleared tonight," Oliver said.

"I'll have to talk to Simon before I know when and where I'm going and how long I'll be gone. They say the phone should be fixed in a couple of days."

"Well, Minnie loves keeping Sammy. She's offered to keep Nita June's boys if she has to go to jail."

"They won't put her in jail. They're saying it was an accident. Thad's very sensitive about abuse."

"Strange how it's all working out. I hope Simon has good news about Abby," Oliver said.

"I have no doubts. If he hasn't found her by now, he's on her trail. He'll find her soon, though it may take a while for her to recover from the traumatic experience. She'll be all right. She's got to be. This nightmare has got to end soon."

The nurse caught the doctor before he left for the night.

"I think you need to check on 202."

"Is she worse?"

"Her temperature's down a little. But she jerks a lot. I'm afraid she'll hurt herself."

The doctor felt Priss's pulse, lifted her eyelids and flashed a light on her pupils.

"You say she's having seizures?"

"It's not seizures. More like she's fighting something."

"What did you give her?"

"Only the medication you ordered."

"I'm glad you brought this to my attention. I think there's more wrong here than pneumonia," the doctor said and wrote new orders. "Watch her and call me at home if there's a change. Especially if she comes out of the coma. If you leave before I get here in the morning, explain to the on-duty nurse. Something about this patient bothers me."

"Me, too."

Delores and Delta were up early, still debating what to do about Simon. Delores wanted to call him, tell him the truth. Delta said wait till he returned.

"What if Priss's fiancé belongs to the Mob, he caught her with someone, and has a contract on her?" Delta said.

"You've been watching too much crime TV," Delores said.

"Yeah? Well, you're the first one to mention the mob. And if she was so all-fired happy with this fiancé, how come she was under a bridge with no memory and no clothes?"

"He could be the guy who told her to wait under the light. You know? The one who cooks."

They finally decided to wait till Simon returned. Then, try to find out why the fiancé was looking for her. Surely, both of them could get that information from a P.I.

They set the diner up for the day and were sipping coffee when their first customer came in.

"Hi, Babes. I thought you were going to call me."

Delta looked up and saw Dwight, grinning, wearing a cop uniform.

"Yeah? Well, I thought you was a country singer."

He grinned and said, "I won the Karaoke contest. Does that qualify me as a singer?"

Delores stood at the end of the bar with her mouth open. She picked up a menu and said, "Breakfast anyone?"

"Anything better than this on the menu?" Dwight said, grinning at Delta.

Delores took Delta's arm and pulled her to the kitchen.

"You didn't tell me he was a cop," Delores whispered.

"Yeah? Well, that's because I didn't know. Heck. He may not be a cop. Maybe he's going to a singing-cop contest."

"Find out if he's connected with the law. It's our chance to come clean. Maybe he can give us advice."

"What's this 'us' business? I'm the one's been looking after Priss. What if I confide in this singing-cop-cowboy and he's in co-hoots with your P.I.?"

"He's not my P.I. Not yet, anyway. They can't be in co-hoots. Dwight was with you when you found Priss."

"Then there's no sense in bringing him into it. Maybe he hooked up with the P.I. after he saw Priss. We'll keep our mouths shut until we talk to Simon. Then, if we have problems, I'll call Dwight," Delta said. "I need to learn more about this singing-cop-cowboy, before I confide in him. Like, is he a cop, a singing cowboy, or both?"

"You can't fool me, Delta. I know what you want from the singing-cop-cowboy," Delores said. "And it ain't information."

Simon drove through the hospital parking lot looking at license plates. No Lincoln's from Blount County, TN. He went to admittance and asked if Abby Crowley had been admitted. He knew the answer. She probably still didn't know her name. He showed her photo to a nurse, who passed it around. No one had seen the woman in the photo. He explained that she was missing, left a photo and his business card. This sort of thing rarely helped, but didn't hurt.

The Murphy police hadn't heard anything about a missing woman. They were most cooperative, made copies of Abby's photo, put them in the squad cars, and posted them all over town. With a good day's work behind him, Simon pointed his car in the direction of the Sunset Diner.

Chapter Twenty-Two

Delores worked double-duty, giving Delta time with Dwight. She picked up bits and pieces of their conversation, which was mostly flirting, wisecracks, and laughing. Nothing serious going on there, except a budding romance. Maybe Delta was analyzing him before revealing information about her situation.

She was nervous, to say the least, but alert, watching the door, afraid Simon would appear any minute. In the short time she had known Delta she had learned to be ready for anything. When the dinner crowd started coming in, Dwight put the police hat on his shaved head and said goodbye to Delta.

Without a word, Delta went to the grill and started turning out orders like a professional cook. When the customers were served, Delores went to the kitchen.

"Well? Is he a cop? Did you ask his advice?"

"He's a cop from Knoxville and I didn't tell him anything. We have a date this weekend."

"You're going out with a cop? Aren't you concerned that he'll find out about your situation?"

"It never hurts to have a cop on your side."

"I'm not sure on your side is where you want him. So, you two are going out where?"

"He's taking me to hear him sing."

"Another Karaoke contest?"

"Church."

"He's singing in church?" Delores shook her head. "I don't see how this will help your situation."

Delta grinned.

"Get your mind out of the gutter. I mean, what are you going to do about Priss?"

"When I finish cleaning up, I'm going to visit her in the hospital. Maybe she'll be well enough to go with us to church."

"If I were you, I'd tell Dwight the whole story and get his advice on what to do."

"Yeah? Well, you ain't me. If you were, you'd know it's not a crime to help a woman who can't remember who she is."

"What are you going to tell Simon when he comes back?"

"*If* he comes back, I won't tell him anything," Delta said.

"No. You probably won't be here. Maybe I should be asking what am I going to tell him."

"Find out why he's hunting Priss before you tell him anything. He said she could be in danger. Did it occur to you that Mr. Simon P.I. and the fiancé may be her only danger?"

"I hadn't thought about that."

"Yeah? Well, you should think about it. You can't trust anybody these days. You've got to learn not to worry so much."

"Maybe I should learn to dye gray hair. Mine's been turning by the minute since you and Priss walked in this place."

Simon passed the hospital as he left Murphy. He thought about stopping again. He decided against it. Leaving the photos and his phone number was all he could do, short of looking in every patient's room. They frowned on that in hospitals.

He stopped at a convenient store, bought two packs of peanut butter crackers and a large diet soda to tide him over until supper at the Sunset Diner. He really wanted to get to know Delores. Business first. He would bet a steak dinner that she knew more than she was telling. If he played his cards right, his personal interest in Delores might help with the business at hand. And, vice versa.

Thirty minutes later, he turned off the car radio and pulled in at the Sunset Diner. The parking lot was packed. He would have to wait till the dinner crowd left before trying to talk to Delores. He walked through the parking lot looking for Blount County license plates.

No luck.

In a wooded area to the side he found a road that curved and ended at a railed entrance to a room behind the diner. May be where Delores lives. Or, where she hides people. Moving closer to a dim light coming from the room's window, he bumped into a car. He turned on his flashlight and saw a green Lincoln Continental with a Blount County tag. *Bingo.*

He knew if he confronted Delta, who was probably inside, or Delores, who apparently knew about the whole escapade, they probably wouldn't tell him anything.

His stomach growled. Too bad. Forget dinner tonight.

He drove his Caddy slowly down the road behind the diner. The tail pipe crunched against the under-brush as he parked in bushes where he could watch the Lincoln. He got out, broke off a few limbs and covered the hood of his Caddy.

In darkness he fumbled in the front seat, found the second pack of peanut butter crackers and the half-empty diet soda and leaned back. *Okay, Lincoln. Take me to Abby.*

Zack had helped Oliver convert their back bedroom into a romper room. Sammy, Frank, and Billy were back there, having a great time with the toys Sammy had brought from Zack's house.

"You leaving right away?" Oliver said.

"I'm still waiting to hear from Simon," Zack said. "I'll call before I leave, even if it's the middle of the night. I'm leaving Sammy with you tonight to see how it works out."

"If Minnie had any say, she'd keep all three of the boys permanently. Heard any more about Nita June?" Oliver said.

"Thad said all the D.A. wanted was an official statement."

"Do they know why Frank's finger prints were on the gun?"

"Apparently, the boy picked up the gun to protect his mother, not knowing his father was already dead. Investigators say the direction of the wound to the chest proved the gun went off when it fell to the floor. There was only one bullet fired, so it makes perfect sense. Under the circumstances, Thad is more concerned with how all this will affect the boys. "

"Don't worry about Sammy, or anything else. I've got your Christmas shopping list. We'll wrap the presents and decorate your house. Maybe Abby will be home to help decorate the tree. The weather man says we might have a white Christmas."

"Frankly, I've had enough ice and snow," Zack said. "But whatever the good Lord drops is okay by me."

They went to the kitchen where Zelphie and Minnie were preparing cookies and hot chocolate for the boys. Zack pecked each woman on the cheek and told them he was leaving, then went to the romper room and sat down in the rocking chair. Sammy dropped his tractor, climbed up in Zack's lap and put his arms around the big man's neck.

"Don't worry, Zack. Mama's Angel is watching her."

For the first time, he said Mama instead of Mommy. He was growing up and becoming a real Tennessean.

"Who told you that, Son?"

"Zelphie. She said we all got an Angel. Minnie said you got one too. And Mama's Angel is gonna tell your Angel where to find her. Is that right, Zack?"

"That's right. You'll be okay till I get back, won't you?"

"Yeah. We're gonna be real busy getting ready for Mama. Minnie said we're gonna put up lights and decorate her house. Then we're gonna decorate our house."

Our house. Zack choked up and cleared his throat.

"Oliver said we're gonna put so many lights on our house, you can see them from the valley. He said you'll be surprised when you get home. And we're gonna cut our very own tree from the woods. I've never done that before. Can I pick the tree?"

"I don't see why not," Zack said, and looked up at Oliver who was listening to the conversation. "You hear that Oliver? Sammy wants to pick the tree."

Oliver, leaning on the wall with his arms folded across his chest, smiled and said, "I'll bet he can pick a good one."

"I'm gonna pick one as tall as the ceiling. Do you think Santa Clause knows where I am?"

"Didn't you send a letter telling him where you live now?"

"Yeah, that's right. I forgot."

"Don't worry if I don't call everyday. Okay?"

"I won't worry, Zack. You'll have your hands full. Minnie told me that. Me and her and Oliver are gonna buy you a present to put under the tree. And you know what? I'm gonna buy a very special present for Mama. You think she will be surprised?"

Zack wanted to boo-hoo like a baby. Big boys don't cry.

"She'll be surprised and happy, Sammy. And she'll be very, very proud of you."

Instead of driving home, Zack went to church. Word was, a new preacher would be starting on Christmas Eve.

He sat on the back pew in the quietness, never so filled with love, sadness and happiness, all at the same time. No need to say anything. God knew what he wanted. God knew what he needed. From somewhere deep inside, a message came to him, almost like someone speaking. *It's all taken care of.*

After the DA got a statement from Nita June, O'Dell and Anderson took her home. Anderson stayed in the car while O'Dell walked her to the door.

"I'm glad you decided to leave the boys with Minnie for the night. You want us to stay with you?"

"I'll be okay. Ya'll done enough."

"I can take Anderson home and come back," O'Dell said.

"Ya' been a real good friend, Pete. But, if ya' don't mind, I'd like t' be alone tonight," Nita June said.

"I don't go to work until late tomorrow. Mind if I come in the morning? I can take you to pick up the boys."

"I've got the truck."

"Then, I'll come make sure it's running good, Nita."

"I like how you call me Nita. I git tired of two names."

"I'll see you in the morning. Want me to bring breakfast?"

"I would really like some Honey Buns," she said.

"Honey Buns it is. And coffee," he said.

"I'll make the coffee," she said, opened the door and turned on the light.

"Sure you'll be okay here tonight?" he said.

"I'll be jus' fine."

"I really do want to help you," he said.

"You're the only man's ever offered t' help me, Pete. So, ain't nothin' wrong with ya' if I'm a bit skeptic."

Pete smiled and said, "Goodnight, Nita."

In your shoes, who wouldn't be skeptic?

When they finished cleaning the kitchen, Delta said, "What happened to Simon, P.I.? He was probably shooting you a line of bull. I'll bet you never see him again."

"This isn't bull," she said, holding up Abby's photo.

"Forget him. Want to go with me to visit Priss?"

"Visiting hours are over."

"Pooh on visiting hours. You coming or what?"

"No. I'm going to bed. Your shenanigans wear me out."

"Yeah? Well, I think you're waiting around in case Mr. Simon P.I. shows up," Delta said and headed to her car.

Just as the cranking of her car woke Simon, his cell phone rang. *Smuck. I forgot to turn the stupid thing off.*

"Thought I'd let you know my phone's working," Zack said.

"Can't talk now," Simon whispered and continued without giving Zack a chance to respond. "I'm in pursuit. Things are getting hot. I'll call you in a few hours. I'm turning off the cell phone now." He hung up, watched the Lincoln pull out and turn toward Murphy. He took off in pursuit as camouflage brush fell from the Caddy's hood.

The Lincoln stopped in the Murphy hospital parking lot. A woman fitting Delta's description got out and went in the back door of the hospital.

This woman doesn't waste time checking in. She visits in the middle of the night, goes directly to the room. Probably Abby's room. And she'll likely stay as long as she wants without anyone knowing she's here.

He started through the door. A nurse was coming in his direction. He jumped back and watched the nurse go in a room. A few seconds later she came out and went down the hall. By now, the woman from the Lincoln was gone. She probably took the stairs. Darting through the stairway door, he heard footsteps going up. He reached the platform just in time to see the woman step into the hallway and go in room 202. Looking both ways, he tiptoed to the room and paused outside. He cracked the door and listened to a voice having a conversation with someone named Priss, who wasn't saying anything. He stepped in the room and stood outside the curtain pulled around the bed. Peeking through the crack in the curtain, he saw the woman from the Lincoln in a chair. Abby was in the bed. She looked like a sleeping ghost. He went inside the curtain, and then jerked it back together. The woman whirled around.

"Hello," he said.

"You're not a doctor. What are you doing in here?"

"I'm Simon Freely. And, you must be Delta."

Chapter Twenty-Three

Simon ain't some dummy you can just handle. He's a pro from the word go. That's what Delores had said. Delta knew she was caught red-handed. She had to out-smart this so-called pro.

"Simon, huh? The Mafia's right hand man."

"And I'm gonna break both your legs if you don't tell me what's going on here."

Well, that's not what she expected.

"So you admit it."

"I'm not admitting anything." Simon flashed his I.D.

"Huh! You probably had that made at a corner photo shop."

"Please tell me she's not in a coma," Simon said.

"What's it to you?"

"Tell me! What's wrong with Abby?"

"Who's Abby?"

"Cut the crap, Delta. I'm hungry. I'm tired. And I'm not going to play your cat and mouse game. I can call the police, or you can start talking to me."

"Police? They can't do nothing to me. All I've done is try to help Priss get her memory back."

"Her name is Abby. Look, Delta. You obviously care about her, or you wouldn't be trying to protect her. Let's take this conversation outside so we won't disturb her. She looks like she needs rest," Simon said and took Delta's arm.

She jerked her arm away. "Don't man-handle me. I'm coming, 'cause you're right. We got plenty to talk about."

"You bet we do. Let's go somewhere private. I'll buy you a cup of coffee."

"How generous. Your car or mine?" Delta said.

"We'd better take mine. The police are looking for yours."

Simon inhaled a cheeseburger and fries while Delta told him the whole story from finding Abby to putting her in the hospital with pneumonia and giving her Delores's name.

"You gave her Delores's name?"

"Well, yeah. I had to do something. She didn't know who she was and I could hardly give her my name. Besides, he's Delores's doctor."

"So, she has pneumonia, but still no memory," Simon said.

"That's right. I went to work at Delores's diner to pay the hospital bill," Delta said.

Simon threw back his head and roared.

"What's so all-fired funny about me working to pay Priss's, I mean Abby's hospital bill?"

"Zack's gonna love this." Simon shook his head and continued to laugh.

"Who's Zack and what's he gonna love?"

"Zack Cole. Abby's fiancé. The guy who's moving heaven and earth to find her."

"*The* Zack Cole. Like in CCI?"

"That's the one. You know him?"

"Crap. Everybody in the computer world knows Zack Cole. Or, knows of him. That's who's hunting Abby? One of the richest men in the U. S. of A.?"

"He's the one. That's why your working to pay Abby's hospital bill struck me as funny."

"I was gonna apply for a job with CCI after I got canned. I hadn't got around to it when I met Abby."

"You in computers?"

"I'm a whiz. If you'd seen me at the diner, you'd have known right off that I'm no cook. Nor waitress."

"We're getting off track here. Do you think you can sit still and shut up long enough for me to tell Abby's story and why she lost her memory?"

"It's past my bed time. But If I can have one of those cheeseburgers, fries, and some more coffee, you got a deal."

Simon waved for the waitress, who brought food and a pot of coffee. It was empty by the time Simon finished his story.

"You see, Delta. Because of Zack's position, we thought someone might have kidnapped her for ransom. That's why someone very reliable has to be with Sammy at all times."

"Jesus. She's got a kid and don't even know it. I've got to go tell her about all this," Delta said.

"Don't be too hasty. From what I understand, in medical terms she probably has post-traumatic stress, which is causing her memory loss. Hearing the wrong thing at the wrong time could be dangerous. If she remembers too much, too soon, she could go further into shock. Before we do anything, the doctor needs to know the whole story. First, I'm calling Zack. He's nearly out of his mind and needs to know I've found her and she's alive. I won't tell him where she is till I talk to the doctor. Can I trust you to go to the diner and wait in case I need you?"

"Well, yeah. No way I'm walking out of this story just when it's gettin' good. I gotta' know how this baby ends."

"You're a jewel, Delta. I've got a feeling you'll be working for CCI before the end of the month."

"No kidding?"

"You can probably name your ticket."

"Anything else you want me to do?"

"You can tell Delores that I'm the greatest guy you've ever met and she should definitely go out with me."

"It'll be my pleasure, Mr. Simon, P.I. If, and only if, you tell the police not to stop the old Lincoln Continental with the Blount County tags."

Zack had been on pin and needles since he interrupted Simon's surveillance. He had never felt so helpless in his life. Everything that had happened lately confirmed what his dad and mom had told him long ago. *All the money in the world can't buy peace, contentment, happiness, and most of all, love.*

He had moved from the desk chair, to the couch, to the bed where he laid staring at the ceiling. At midnight, he put the portable phone by the shower where he could hear it, and stepped in the hot water, hoping to drench away his stress. Then he turned on the cold water to wake up. Trying to decide what he might need if Simon called and wanted him to leave immediately, he packed an overnight bag.

Leaning back in his lounger, he watched the news until he got sleepy. That wouldn't do. He went to the computer and sent e-mail memos to his CEOs. Then he thought of Abby.

When I find you, I'm asking you to marry me. Right on the spot. But, maybe not. What if you don't remember me? What do you remember? Sammy. Of course. But, if you remember him at all, you'll remember him dead. That's what caused you to walk off. What do you love about this place? What makes you smile? Where did you go when you were sad, or happy? You always went to the rose garden. The White Meidilands.

Determined to stay awake, he put on his coat, grabbed the phone and went out on the balcony. The cold mountain air ought to do the trick. Down in the valley, Soda Creek was lit up with Christmas decorations. The stars above twinkled against a clear sky. The sun would be up in a few hours. He went back inside.

Will you want a big wedding? A Justice of the Peace? What if you won't marry me? What if you hate me when you remember?

By the dim light from the refrigerator he poured water in the coffee maker. He was sitting at the breakfast bar listening to the water drip through the filter when the phone rang.

"I've found Abby," Simon said.

"Thank God. Is she okay?"

"She alive. She has pneumonia. Doesn't remember anything. I just wanted to be sure you have someone to keep Sammy. Can you be ready to leave on a moment's notice?"

"I'm ready now. Tell me where to go. Where is she?"

"Trust me, old buddy. It's not time yet. Sit by the phone. It's almost over. I'll call back in a few hours with directions," Simon said, and hung up.

Zack stared at the phone still in his hand. He didn't care if it was three in the morning. He called Oliver.

"I don't know when I'll be back. But looks like she may be home for Christmas."

"Stay as long as it takes," Oliver said. "Don't worry about a thing."

"She's not out of the woods, yet. Keep your fingers crossed. And Oliver," Zack said, choking up. "Pray."

"We'll all be praying, Zack."

"Will you tell Nita June? And, call Thad. Use the number I gave you. It's his home phone."

"I'll take care of it, Zack."

Zack hung up and bowed his head.

Oh, God. My cup runneth over.

He cried and cried. Out loud, like a baby. There was no one to hear. He wanted to sit on the back pew in church. But he dared not leave the phone.

A nurse rushed to Simon. She had recognized Abby from her photo and had been trying to get in touch with him.

"I found her. I'm here to talk to her doctor," he said.

After the doctor heard about Abby's misfortunes, he made an appointment with Zack, who arrived in ninety minutes.

"I see you brought roses. Is she familiar with this color?" the doctor said to Zack.

"They're her favorites."

"Good. That's most valuable. It's important that you understand what we're dealing with before you go in to see her," the doctor said, and proceeded to explain.

"The symptoms of amnesia, or loss of memory, especially the inability to recognize ideas represented by words, are varied and of different types. Ante-retrograde amnesia is loss of memory directly following severe shock or trauma. Auditory Amnesia is an inability to recognize the spoken word. Abby doesn't have that. She understands what we say. In retrograde amnesia, memory of all previous events is obliterated. Sometimes those incidents occurring after an accident are also effaced, called post-traumatic amnesia. The latter is of variable duration and is a yardstick of the severity of the shock or injury.

Amnesia may be partial, for instance, losing one's memory for sounds, names, or colors. Or it may be general with a loss of the greater part of memory. It frequently involves a sudden emotional conflict and memory will begin to return when the conflict is resolved. Doctors often find it difficult to decide in these cases whether or not the inability to remember is actual or simulated. If someone is simply refusing to remember, the diagnosis is difficult. Cases are on record of people who have had as many as five periods of complete loss of memory with subsequent recovery. Occasionally, a person can't recall his name or address. Psychiatrists believe that such persons suffer from amnesia because of their inability to cope with situations, which apparently were so painful that the only solution was to deny their identity. I believe that's what happened with Abby, whereas, even in total amnesia certain habits are remembered, such as writing, walking, and reading."

"Then I should be careful what I say to her," Zack said.

"Yes. Very careful. Just follow her lead. I'll be beside you during the initial meeting. Before you see her, you must meet Delta. She's been with Abby since she ran away from the Maryville hospital. Her being with you for the initial meeting is important because she may be the only one Abby recognizes."

Simon opened the door and Delta came in.

"Mr. Cole, I'm so glad to meet you. If I had known…"

Zack reached out both arms, embraced Delta, and said, "Thank you for looking after Abby. Call me Zack."

Delta hugged him tight, then pushed back and looked him in the eye. "Do you cook?"

Everybody in the room chuckled.

"He's the best cook in the country," Simon said.

"Why?" Zack said.

"Honey, she already remembers you. Who wouldn't remember a man who cooks? Did you tell her to wait on a bench under a street light?"

"Yes. I told her to wait there while I went back to get Sammy. Is that important?"

"Well, yeah. The only words she's said since I've known her were about you. This is gonna be so good. She remembers you. You're just what she needs to pull her out of this mess."

"I have a few questions. Let's say she doesn't remember me. What then?" Zack said to the doctor.

"You act the same whether or not she remembers. Follow her lead," the doctor said.

"What if she remembers Sammy?" Zack asked.

"That will be tricky. You see, you didn't cause her condition. Chances are, she'll remember you. Delta said she has talked about you without saying your name. When she sees you, she'll probably remember your name. Believing she had lost Sammy, and then being abducted, triggered the amnesia. If she mentions Sammy, say he's okay, but don't say his name until she does. Otherwise, avoid that subject," the doctor said.

"To be frank, doctor, I can't wait to see her. But, I'm scared to death. Anything I say could trigger something awful and do her more harm than good," Zack said.

"That's a perfectly normal feeling. Remember, I'll be there to interrupt if things get risky," the doctor said.

Simon put his hand on Zack's shoulder and said, "You're almost home, buddy."

"Now, if you two will step out, I'd like a few moments alone with Zack," the doctor said.

"No problem, Doc," Simon said, took Delta's arm and led her from the room.

"I think it's important that you know, according to the records I received from Maryville, Abby was not raped. That's why I feel so strongly that her memory loss was the result of believing she had lost Sammy, and the abduction."

Zack put his hand to his mouth, dabbed at his watery eyes, then took a deep breath. "Thank you. Most doctors would have forgotten to convey that information."

The doctor opened the door.

"Okay. Are we ready?"

They walked down the hall together. The doctor opened the door. Zack saw Abby and backed into the hall.

"Go on in, Delta," the doctor said. "Don't say a word about Zack. We'll be in momentarily."

"She's so pale and skinny. Are you sure she's going to be okay?" Zack said to the doctor.

"She's very weak from pneumonia. But she's going to be fine," the doctor said.

"Hey, ole buddy," Simon said. "The girl of your dreams needs you to be strong."

"Right," Zack said, and walked slowly into the room where Delta sat on the right side of the bed, quiet as a mouse.

Abby turned her head on the pillow and saw Zack standing by her bed, holding the roses.

Chapter Twenty-Four

"You came back," Abby said.

"Yes. I came back," Zack said. He ached to hold her. But he was afraid to touch her. Almost afraid to speak.

"I'm sorry I moved from the light," she said.

"That's okay. I found you," Zack said, and smiled.

"What'd I tell you? A man who cooks can do anything."

Abby looked at Delta. Then turned back to Zack and smiled. "Delta said you'd find me."

"That's the first time I've ever seen her smile," Delta whispered to Simon, unable to hold back her tears. Simon put his arm around her shoulder and gave her a handkerchief.

"Did you unplug the iron?" Abby said.

"Yes, I unplugged the iron," Zack said. *My God. She's back in Chicago.*

Abby's brow wrinkled. She looked away, then back at Zack. "Did you save him, Zack? Is he okay?"

She said Zack. His heart almost jumped out of his chest.

"He's fine, Abby." *Christ. I shouldn't have said her name.*

"I'm Abby." Her face went blank. Then she smiled at Delta. "I'm Abby." With a weak hand she took the roses and brought them to her nose. "White Meidilands. My favorites." She closed her eyes. "Is he in Paradise, Zack? Is he safe in Paradise?"

Zack froze. *Did she mean Paradise, like in Heaven? What am I suppose to say now? Be careful. She hasn't said Sammy's name. Don't say his name. God help me.*

"He's safe, Abby. He's safe at home," Zack said.

"He's safe in Paradise." She smiled at Zack, reached out and

177

held his hand. Suddenly, her face went blank as if she didn't know where she was. She turned her head, stared out the window for a moment, and closed her eyes.

The doctor opened the door and motioned for everyone to leave the room.

"That was perfect. Better than I expected. But she's had enough for the first meeting," the doctor said. "Will you be back tomorrow, Zack?"

"I'm not leaving. I'm staying outside this door till she's well enough to go home."

"Yeah? Well, I'm heading for the diner as fast as I can. Delores won't believe all this," Delta said.

"Tell her I'll see her later tonight. That okay with you, Zack?" Zack's bewildered face answered the question. "Right. Tell her I'll see her soon."

"She'll be glad to hear that. I told her what you said, Mr. P.I. She agrees." Delta turned to Zack. "Zack Cole. God should 'a made a man like you for every woman on earth. I'll be back tomorrow," she said and left.

The doctor said to Zack, "I know you want to stay. And, I understand. But there's nothing more you can do now. She needs rest and time to consume this. Go home. Prepare Sammy."

"Should I bring him with me tomorrow?"

"I think we should wait. We're treading on very thin ice. This Paradise thing has me concerned," the doctor said.

"Me, too," Zack said.

"But the roses did the trick, huh, Doc?" Simon said.

"That was the perfect touch."

"Thank you, doctor. I'll see you tomorrow. If you think I should come."

"Visit every day. Her recovery depends on it. For the next couple of visits, I'll be in the room with you. Here's my schedule. I'll see you tomorrow."

"Thanks, Doctor," Zack said.

"Come on, Buddy. I'm anxious to sit on the mountain and relax while you grill me a steak for supper," Simon said.

Before seeing Sammy, who was in the romper room with Frank and Billy, Zack talked to Nita, Minnie, Zelphie and Oliver.

"Taking the roses was genius, Zack," Zelphie said.

"Lucky some were blooming in the greenhouse," Zack said.

"When will you take Sammy to see her?" Oliver said.

"The doctor doesn't think it's a good idea right now. She asked if he was safe in Paradise. That concerned us. She may be referring to Paradise as Heaven, still thinking Sammy's dead, because she didn't say his name. Not once."

"What did you tell her?" Minnie said.

"I said *he* was safe at home."

"No, no, no, Zack," Nita June said. "Paradise is what she calls your place."

"She never told me that," Zack said.

"The first time I met her, she said yore place wuz so much like Heaven, she named it Paradise. That's yore home, Zack."

"Not without Abby, it's not. But knowing that changes everything. Thank you, Nita," he said, squeezing her hand. "I must call the doctor right away. He'll be thrilled. First, I'll tell Sammy I've found his mother. Then Simon and I are going home. I promised him a grilled steak tonight."

"You'll do no such thing," Minnie said. "You're too tired, stressed out, and overwhelmed to cook. You and Simon will eat here. I've got enough food to feed an army. We were about to put it on the table. Go talk to Sammy."

Oliver grinned. "I'm afraid you'll have to grill later."

"Okay by me." Simon went to the stove and peeked under a pot lid. "What's for supper, Minnie?"

"You get out of here till I put it on the table," she said, slapping his hand.

He grinned and followed his buddy to the romper room.

Sammy jumped up and threw his arms around Zack.

"I missed you, Zack. Did you find Mama?"

179

"Simon found her, Sammy."

"Then Mama's Angel must know Simon's Angel, too."

"I think all the Angels know each other," Simon said.

"Did Mama come home to see me?"

"No, Son. Your mama is really, really sick. She needs to get better before she comes home," Zack said.

"Oh. Does she have a real bad headache?"

"She has a real bad heartache, Sammy. It's very hard to explain. You trust me, don't you?"

Sammy put his arms around Zack's neck and kissed his cheek.

"I love you, Zack."

Those words from a child meant total trust.

Snow was falling when Abby walked away from the hospital holding Zack's arm.

"I remember the first time I saw this car," Abby said as they got in the white Ferrari.

"At the Knoxville airport," Zack said.

"Shortly after I got my driver's license, I was driving it and got lost on a back road in Soda Creek."

"You didn't tell me that."

"I didn't tell you a lot of things I should have," she said and looked back to see if the others were following. "Is that Simon's car back there?"

"He's directly behind us."

"As always, you've made everything work out beautifully for everyone. Inviting Simon, Dwight, Delta, and Delores to spend the holidays with us was a wonderful idea. Your generosity, goodness, and ability to solve problems are just a few of the many reasons I love you so much."

Zack's heart skipped. "What did you say?"

"I said…"

"Never mind." He turned on the blinker and pulled off the road. Checking the rear view mirror, he watched Simon pull over behind him.

"I've put this off long enough," he said. Taking Abby's face in his hands, he kissed her, long and gentle.

"Wow," Abby said when he finally let go. "I doubt that I'll ever forget that." He kissed her again, and again.

"Why didn't you tell me you loved me before?"

"I tried. While you were away on trips, I'd plan how I was going to say it. But, when you got home, other things got in the way. Plus, I didn't want you to think my love was confused with gratitude. Of course, I'm grateful for all you've done for Sammy and me. But, I love everything about you, Zack."

"I love you, Abby. God, how I love you. I have so much to tell you."

"We have a lifetime to talk," Abby said.

The passengers in the car behind them cheered as Simon blinked his headlights.

"It's about time," Simon said.

"You got that right," Delta blurted from the back seat.

"There's gotta be a song written about this," Dwight said.

Simon pulled up beside Zack's car and rolled down the window. "Take your time. We'll see you on the mountain."

From the valley Abby could see the Christmas decorations on Zack's house.

"How beautiful. It truly is Paradise. Our Paradise."

"I like that. *Our Paradise,*" Zack said.

"It's like a city to itself up there. Do you always decorate so much at Christmas?"

"No. This year is special. Sammy helped decorate," Zack said, and pulled onto the road that led up to his home. "I see Oliver scraped the road so we'd have no problem getting up."

When they turned in the gate, Abby said, "Oh, my. It takes my breath away. More than ever."

Lights were strung everywhere, lighting up the yard, which was filled with people playing in the snow. A huge snowman facing the road held a big sign that said, "Welcome home, Abby."

"Who are all these people?"

"Friends, citizens of Soda Creek. Look who's standing by the snowman," Zack said.

She jumped from the car and ran to Sammy. Tears soaked her face as she knelt on the snow and threw her arms around her son.

"Don't cry, Mama," he said, as the crowd cheered. He took Abby's hand on one side, Zack's on the other, and led them in the house where the crowd gathered in the long front room. A buffet was set up with more food than Abby had ever seen in one place.

"See the tree? I picked it 'specially for you from the woods. Oliver cut it down with his chain saw. You like it?"

"It's the most beautiful tree I've ever seen," Abby said, observing the Angel on top that touched the ceiling. More importantly, she'd never seen her son so happy.

"Look at the presents, Mama. I got this one for you. But you can't open it 'til morning. Zack said I'd get lots more tonight, 'cause Santa Clause knows where I live now."

The crowd followed as Sammy pulled Zack and Abby outside through the snow to the green house.

"The roses in the garden won't bloom in winter. So, me and Zack growed these white ones for you cause you like them best."

Abby put her hands to her chest.

Everyone from the welcome party went to the Christmas Eve service. Zack took his usual pew in the back, with Sammy between him and Abby. The small church was crowded with people standing in the aisles and around the back. Even Thad and the deputies were there.

"I know you have a rather sentimental attachment to the back seat, Brother Cole. But it won't work tonight," the deacon said, and led Zack and Abby and Sammy to the front.

After a welcome home speech for Abby, and the congregation sang Joy to the World, the deacon introduced the new minister.

A neat, slim man of medium height, wearing a navy-blue suit walked from the back of the church and stood at the podium.

Abby froze. Zack put his arm around her.

"Merry Christmas, everybody," the preacher said.

The audience responded with the same.

"My name is Larry Alday. On the precious eve of our Lord and Savior's birth, I'm living proof that the Father still works in mysterious ways. He put a judge in front of me that gave me a year's probation doing community service. I told him I wanted to preach the word of God. He told me you needed a preacher. See how God works His wonders? He puts people in your path to change your life. And, what's even more mysterious, most of the time we don't even know it's happening. Tonight, right here in front of God and everybody, I give praise and glory to God for not only sending me a Savior to save my soul, but for putting a person in my path to save my life on earth. It wasn't an easy task the Lord laid on this person. She went through hell on earth to change this old sinner."

He stepped from the pulpit and stood in front of Abby.

"Thank you, Abby, for being God's instrument that changed my life."

There wasn't a dry eye in the congregation as Abby stood and nervously shook Larry's hand. He wasn't satisfied with a mere handshake. He embraced her and said, "You are indeed an Angel."

In front of the podium a halo surrounded the bouquet of White Meidilands from Zack's greenhouse.

* * *

183